# FORBIDDEN PLOT

## WRITTEN BY;

## CYRIL PRECIOUS.

# <u>ACKNOWLEDGEMENT</u>

I'M FOREVER GRATEFUL TO MY CREATOR, FOR THE INSPIRATION TO COMPILE THIS BOOK AND FOR THE BLESSINGS OF MAKING THIS A SUCCESSFUL PROJECT. I SPECIALLY WANT TO THANK EVERYONE THAT HAS PURCHASED A COPY OF THIS BOOK WITH THEIR HARD EARNED MONEY; WITHOUT YOUR SUPPORT, THIS WON'T HAVE GAINED THE RECOGNITION, IT DESERVES. THANK YOU EVERYONE THAT KEEPS SUPPORTING MY WORK, ESPECIALLY, MY FAMILY AND WELLWISHERS.

## ACT 1, SCENE ONE

(One could tell the weather in Ala Umu Obodo is a chilly weather, the dust keeps making their presence felt, as if they've become a living thing overnight. Anyone who frequently tours the eastern part of west Africa, mostly during the end and turn of the year, would easily tell that "Harmattan", has taking Centre stage).

**UDO.** Nne m, is it proper for me as a man to wear waist beads?

**ULOMA.** It is not proper, my son; waist beads are mostly worn by females, and mainly considered feminine.

**UDO.** Nne m, but is it possible for a man to grow breast?

**ULOMA.**  That's an abomination! Don't ever say that with this mouth of yours; it isn't right, my son.

**UDO.**  Nne m, can a man have feelings?

**ULOMA.**  Of course, you're human; the feeling of love is the mutual bond, we all share together.

**UDO.**  Does that mean I can fall in love, with my fellow man?

**ULOMA.**  Udo! Udo!! Don't ever say this outside the walls of this house! And why are you asking such disturbing questions?

**UDO.**  Nne m, it is nothing but a mix-up, which I want to clarify, once and for all.

**ULOMA.**  Udo, I agree that you've reached the age to make your own decisions; which makes you ready to assume your responsibility as a man. However, you have to know there are some things that are forbidden in this land, **"Homosexuality"**, is one of them. My son, can you promise me you'll never develop feelings for your fellow man?


(Udo runs off, without giving his honest words as a promise to his mother's request. His mother; who he prefers calling, "Nne m", which means, "My mother", in the lingo used, actually Igbo language).


**ACT 1, SCENE TWO**

**ULOMA.**  Hello Nnamdi, have you seen my son, Udo?

**NNAMDI.**  Not at all, mama. Udo my friend, hasn't passed this route, as far as I can recall.

**ULOMA.**  Ewuchim oo; (a call for God, in the lingo used)! Udo ran from the house this morning, and this is nighttime, still he isn't back; I am worried sick.

**NNAMDI.**  But mama, have you tried looking for him near the Igwe's palace?

**ULOMA.**  At the palace, you say? But what will take Udo over to the king's palace, not like he'd go there to report me for doing nothing to him?

**NNAMDI.**  Mama, I don't know how I'll say this to you, even I, I'm confused.

**ULOMA.**  Nnamdi, if it concerns my son, please you have to spit it out because I'm always interested.

**NNAMDI.**  (Nnamdi breathes heavily, before he spoke up). Well mama, Udo loves roaming around the Igwe's palace to stare at the chest of the Igwe's palace guards; he clearly told me he likes staring at men that are muscular, and he sees no issue staring at them for the whole day. Mama, are you feeling alright, seeing how you're losing your balance?

**ULOMA.**  Nna…mdi, are you telling me nothing but the truth, or you've resorted to playing stupid games, like you two tend to do?

**NNAMDI:**  Mama, I might not have been blessed to see my own mother, but I'll
never lie to you; seeing how you're like a mother figure to me.
How about we go to the palace right now, to see if he's there?

**ULOMA:**  Hmm, you know what, Nnamdi? Take the lead, and let's go.


(The setting of the story is a typical ancient village style; they opt to go to the
palace on their own foot, without envisioning the luxury of looking out for
motorcycle riders, or better yet, calling a cabman).

ACT 2, SCENE THREE


**PALACE GUARD:**  Igwe (it refers to; my king, in the language used)!

**IGWE:**  What is the chaos all about?

**PALACE GUARD:**  Igwe, we found this boy wandering around the palace premises; for a purpose that remains unknown.

**IGWE:**  Free him, guards!

**PALACE GUARD:**  Yes, your majesty.

**IGWE:**  Young man, what's your name and what's your business in my palace?

**PALACE GUARD:**  Will you speak up before the king, and stop trembling?

**UDO:**  My name is …U…D…O.

**IGWE:**  Are you a female disguised as a male; why do you sound so cowardly?

**PALACE GUARD:**  Igwe!

**IGWE:**  What is it again?

**PALACE GUARD:**  Your majesty, he has peed his pants.

(At this point, irritation isn't even a word suitable for expressing the king's mood, because he was so enraged, that he immediately ordered 24 strokes to be unleashed on the young man, called Udo).


**ACT 2, SCENE FOUR**


**PALACE GUARD.**  Igwe! There's a woman outside the palace that claims to be the mother of this boy, who's mercilessly being flogged right now.

**IGWE.**  You mean the mother of this boy that lacks his testicles as a man?

**PALACE GUARD.**  Yes, your Majesty, she is pleading this instant to see her son.

**IGWE.**  Have her come in at once!

(The woman in question was brought before the king immediately).

**IGWE.**  State your name before the Igwe, and did you say this is your son?

**ULOMA.**  My name is Uloma, and he's indeed my son, your majesty; a mother's heart recognizes the tears of her child, even before recognizing his looks.

**IGWE.**  And how old is this son of yours?

**ULOMA:**  Your majesty, he clocked 18, not long ago.

**IGWE:**  Uloma, like you called your name; this boy I see right here is not worthy to be called a man, but rather, a mommy's girl. He can't even take a whip; he cries like a newborn and holds on to his buttocks, like he cherishes it more than any part of his body. Also Uloma, who is your husband?

**ULOMA:**  Your majesty, Udo's father is no more; he tragically left us, without seeing his son grow older.

**IGWE:**  I thought as much, no worthy father will be alive and watch his son grow to become a mommy's girl; women shouldn't be allowed to raise a male child, because he will grow to be a coward that will enslave himself in trying to please a woman, which is simply, intolerable and impossible.

**ULOMA:**  Igwe, please will you order your guards to stop whipping him? I can't stand to watch any longer, for it hurts and breaks my heart so deeply.

**IGWE:**  Woman, how dare you try to fake tears in the presence of your king? I am a proud man that gives zero tolerance to the pretense and cunning ways of a woman. I'll even have my own son stoned to death, if he befriends a son like yours, or behaves as cowardly as your son; right in front of his own mother, who's the Queen. Your son has only received 8 lashes, and I ordered my guards to unleash 24 strokes on him; for lacking his manliness in my presence. Who gave your son, the effrontery to urinate on his own body, in presence of the Igwe? This whipping continues! Let's see if it will help him regain his senses, as a man.

**ULOMA:**  Your majesty, words fail me to plead for your mercy, and please punish us; but let me receive the remaining 16 lashes on his behalf?

**IGWE.**  Woman, your crocodile tears and cock and bull tales, will only make matters worse! Let me remind you, Uloma; nothing is so bad, compared to the fact that it can get even worse. If you can't stand to watch, like you uttered, then it's simple; tell me to pluck out your eyes and I'll give the royal command, so you can very well go blind.

(If there's something, the king was feared for; it's his scary choice of words, which compelled Udo's mother to heartbreakingly and fearfully watch her son get flogged so excruciatingly. In expense of her uncontrollable tears, from every whip, her son endured; till her eyes became as reddish as the color of blood).

**ACT 3, SCENE FIVE**

ULOMA. Nnamdi, please bring him inside so he can lie down on the wooden chair; one can tell he's in severe pains, from the bruises he sustained.

NNAMDI. Mama, but what did Udo do that made Igwe ordered his guards to show no mercy, but whip him brutally?

ULOMA. My son Udo, disgustingly wet the igwe's palace with his urine and that must have been after he was caught staring at the palace guards, just like you notified me.

NNAMDI. Mama, it seems Udo wants to say something; he is trying to get up.

ULOMA. Please, will you assist him, Nnamdi?

UDO. Nne m, please forgive me, I never meant to get into any trouble at the palace.

ULOMA. My son, please lie down, you shouldn't speak now but get some rest; your body must hurt a lot as it is. Nnamdi, will you please stay with him, so I can go fetch some herbs that will help relieve his body pain?

NNAMDI. Mama, I'll gladly stay with him, till you get back. But won't it be too dangerous to go out now, how about you chill till daybreak?

ULOMA. Thank you Nnamdi, but this can't wait at all; also, I won't take long.


**ACT 3, SCENE SIX**

**ULOMA.**  Dede (it refers to; an elder, in the lingo used)! Dede!! Is anyone at home?

**DEDE.**  Onye na acho m na abali a (it means; who's looking for me by this time of the night, in the lingo used)?

**ULOMA.**  It's your niece, Uloma.

**DEDE.**  This is a true surprise! But what brings you to my hut in this ungodly hour, Uloma?

**ULOMA.**  Dede, my son Udo, is the main reason why I can't wait till dawn to visit, nor even bring you your favorite dish; loi loi and ofe ede (this is commonly known as fufu and cocoyam soup).

**DEDE.**  What happened to my great-nephew, Udo?

**ULOMA.**  Hmm, I don't know where to start from, but there's fire on the mountain.

**DEDE.**  Uloma, I've always told you not to beat around the bush in my presence; I'm a man, and we speak straight up.

**ULOMA.**  Can you please forgive me, Dede? It so happens that this matter I want to discuss with you; is one that dries saliva from the mouth of the speaker.

**DEDE.**  Uloma, since this matter is of huge importance, like you claimed; let's go to the backyard, so you can tell me at once, while I keep roasting the yam I brought out to eat.

**ULOMA.**  Dede, Is it not too late to eat?

**DEDE.**  You are right my child, however; the worms of our stomach, knows no time to attack the intestine. No time to waste Uloma, lekwa oche (it directs one to have a seat, in the lingo used). Now can you tell me what worries you deeply?

**ULOMA.**  Dede, I'm scared that my son Udo, is homosexual.

**DEDE.**  Uloma, you are still yet to swallow the water in your mouth, so you can sound more audibly and clearly.

**ULOMA.**  Dede, I fear my son desires his fellow man in a way that a man desires a woman; sexually.

**DEDE.**  Abomination! May the gods forbid! Uloma, do you know the implications of the forbidden act, you just spewed? And do you know this has never being experienced in the long existence of this village?

**ULOMA.**  Dede, this is what scares me the most; I'm yet to see a man feel sexual desires for his fellow man, as well.

**DEDE.**  Biko chere, Uloma (it means; hold on or please wait, in the lingo used). What made you come to this assumption?

**ULOMA.**  Dede, how I wish it's just an assumption, but the thing is; the signs are becoming obvious from his actions and questions. Yesterday, I guess we are already in the early hours of a new day; my son Udo, asked if it is right for a man to grow the breast of a woman?

**DEDE.**  Ihe-aru (it means; an abomination, in the language used)!

**ULOMA.**  Not only that, Dede; Udo roams around the palace daily, to stare at the
naked chest of muscular men, who stands guard at the palace.

**DEDE.**  I si gini (it means; you say what, in the lingo used)?

**ULOMA.**  Dede, that's not all, I'm scared the king has noticed him acting girlish,
as well.

**DEDE.**  Uloma, I cautioned you earlier to speak directly when speaking to me,
and not to beat around the bush.

**ULOMA.**  Dede, Igwe ordered his guards to unleash 24 strokes on Udo's
buttocks, when he shamefully urinated on his body in the presence of
Igwe, after being caught wandering around the palace premises.

**DEDE.**  This is despicable and disgusting! Udo has overdone it this time, how can
he choose to be a coward?

**ULOMA.**  Dede, what got me worried the most is the fact that Udo begged to be
flogged in any other part of his body, except his buttocks; it's just like
my son protects his buttocks as his treasure.

**DEDE.**  Say no more, Uloma; the more you go further, the more I wish to pick up
my machete and go cut Udo's manhood off!

**ULOMA.**  Dede, please don't speak in that tone for it frightens me even more; I
came here, so you can guide me on what to do concerning this issue.

**DEDE.**  Uloma, you are the only child of my late sister, that's why I took you
in like my own daughter; I won't leave you to deal with this matter all
alone. I'll come in the next three days to visit, Udo. I'll have a **man to man**

discussion with him; his father might have tragically passed away immediately after his birth, but there's still a man in the family.

**ULOMA.**  Thank you a lot Dede, I truly wished Udo's father was still with us; maybe Udo would have acted more manly. Do you think he's experiencing this because I'm a woman, and he grew up by my side, so he adopted my feminine behaviors?

**DEDE.**  That's all in your head, my daughter; you have sacrificed a lot as a mother to Udo. Or have you ever taken Udo over to the palace to stare at the palace guards?

**ULOMA.**  May the gods forbid, Dede! I will do no such thing; the only man I've ever set eyes on is Udo's father, and I've never coveted any other man since he died while hunting, 18 years ago.

**DEDE.**  It's alright Uloma, I'll come in three days like I said earlier, to visit Udo.

**ULOMA.**  We shall anticipate your visit, Dede; I need to get going now, because I told them I want to quickly fetch herbs to help relieve Udo's body pain.

**DEDE.**  Hold on Uloma, you said "Them"?

**ULOMA.**  Yes Dede, I meant Udo and his best friend, Nnamdi; who's looking after him on my behalf.

**DEDE.**  Uloma! Uloma!! How many times did I call you?

**ULOMA.**  Dede, it's three times.

**DEDE:**   Meghe anya gi (it means; keep your eyes opened, in the lingo used)!
Uloma, I know Nnamdi is Udo's childhood friend, but it might still be
unwise to leave them all alone. Uloma, "I maara ka o si bido (it means; do
you know how this all started, in the lingo used)"?

**ULOMA:**   Dede, words fail me to explain how this all started.

**ACT 4, SCENE SEVEN**

## Three Days Later

**VILLAGER.**   Ututu oma, Dee (good morning to an elderly person; in the lingo used)!

**DEDE.**   Ya diri gi nma, Nwa m (it is well with you, my child; in the lingo used).

**VILLAGER.**   Dee (an elderly person), where are you going to this morning?

**DEDE.**   My child, I want to go visit my niece Uloma and her son, Udo.

**VILLAGER.**   That's so caring of you; Dee, please take care and send my regards to them.

**DEDE.**   I will my child, and please send my regards to your parents as well, tell them, I'll come visit them when I'm chanced.

(This scene is between a villager and the uncle of Udo's mum, who is on his way to visit his niece, and grandnephew; who is the same person as Udo's mom, Uloma and her son, Udo).

**ACT 4, SCENE EIGHT**

**DEDE.**  Onye no n'ulo, abiala m (it means; who is at home, I've arrived, in the lingo used)?

(Udo's mother rushed out to receive the guest, who is the same person as her uncle).

**ULOMA.**  Dede, please come inside, we've being waiting.

**DEDE.**  My dear Uloma, if there's something I'm renowned for; that's keeping my word. I told you I'll visit you in three days, and here I am. Hope my grandnephew, who's also my grandson, is inside?

**ULOMA.**  Yes Dede, Udo has regained his strength to move around, and he is so happy, you are coming to visit.

**DEDE.**  Uloma, as a man, I prefer striking the iron while it's still hot; so let's go in and face what I came here for, at once!

**ULOMA.**  Please watch your head, Dede; you know Udo and you are the ones with heights, while I'm measured to the height of a bottle.

**DEDE.**  What can I say, Uloma? However, you're a beautiful fair lady, and your son's lookalike both in complexion and good looks.

**ULOMA.**  Udo, come and say your greetings to papa!

**UDO.**  Good morning, Nna anyi (our father).

**DEDE.**  Kedu ka i mere, Udo (it means; how are you doing, in the lingo used)?

**UDO:**  I'm recuperating, Nna anyi.

**DEDE:**  I'm glad to hear that, Udo; however, I came here for another purpose.

**UDO:**  Please do tell me, Nna anyi; I'm all ears.

**DEDE:**  Udo, do you feel sexually attracted to your fellow man?

(The question struck Udo so hard, that he closed his eyes like he had flashbacks).

**ULOMA:**  Udo, please answer papa's question.

**DEDE:**  Woman, if you interrupt this man to man conversation, I'm having with
your son; I'll hit you like you stole from my farmland.

**ULOMA:**  Dede, my apologies, I'll just standstill like a statue, so please don't ask
me to leave.

**DEDE:**  Udo, I'm the closest person you have to a father and grandfather, so trust
me and speak openly; I never tolerate lies. I'll ask again; Udo, do you have
sexual desires for your fellow man?

(Udo kept trembling, biting his upper lip, and he still didn't let a single word slip
out of his mouth, even in his mystified state).

**DEDE:**  Udo, as a man; our patience runs out very fast, and right now, I'm feeling
so enraged by your incompetence to utter a single word, let alone, to dare
stare at me eyeball to eyeball. I'll rephrase the question this time around;
have you seen a woman you desire?

**UDO:**  I haven't seen any, Nna anyi.

**DEDE:**  We are making progress now; so, I'll ask you another question.
Have you had your first time with anyone?

**UDO:**  Nna anyi, I don't under…stand.

**DEDE:**  Udo, I don't bite, so I don't see why you're shaky in my presence, like
I want to devour you. What I mean by, "Your first time"; is have you had
sexual intercourse, or your first sexual escapade?

**UDO:**  I haven't had at all with anyone.

**DEDE:**  Good, Udo; so why do you visit the palace daily, like you're a member
of Igwe's cabinet? Udo, if you take your eyes away from mine again,
I'll slap you so hard that your senses will come back to you, as if they left in
the first place.

**UDO:**  I'm sorry, Nna anyi.

**DEDE:**  Now, answer me straight up; why do you visit Igwe's palace daily?

**UDO:**  I don't know why, Nna anyi; the impulse comes on me so strongly that I
can't reject the excitement to go over to the Igwe's palace.

**DEDE:**  Udo, continue; when you get to the Igwe's palace, what's your next
action?

**UDO:**  I can't say it, Nna anyi.

(Udo unexpectedly received a brain formatting slap from a man, who he sees as
his grandfather).

**DEDE:**  Udo, I slapped you because it seems you don't know the forbidden act,
you're getting involved in. Now, I'll ask you a question that disgusts and

annoys me at the same time; have you been staring at the chest of muscular men that stands guard at the palace?

**DEDE.** Speak up! Speak up!!

(Udo runs off immediately, as fast as his legs could carry him, after he felt threatened, from the man to man discussion, he's having with his mom's uncle).

**ULOMA.** Dede, you shouldn't have slapped him. I know my son; he must be so terrified right now. (Udo's mom made her voice heard to her uncle, with tears rolling down her cheeks).

**DEDE.** Why are you crying, Uloma? I'm beginning to also see reasons to believe that the home training you instilled in this boy, which can be seen as nothing to write about; is the same reason why he is turning out to be useless, and a big shame to our ancestors! I'll be on my way now, but get prepared, Uloma; because we'll go visit Ezemmuo, first thing tomorrow morning. Have I made myself clear?

**ULOMA.** I'll do whatever it takes as a mother, to see that my son regains his masculinity.

**DEDE.** Not like you have a choice, Uloma; so dry those stupid tears of yours, and go look for a rope to use in tying and dragging your son back home, before he makes his foolishness known to everyone in this village.

**ULOMA.** Dede, I will still thank you for coming over to visit us.

**DEDE.** Uloma, "O biara ije nwe ula" (it means; someone that came on a journey, also have to go back, in the lingo used).

**ACT 4, SCENE NINE**

(Udo is still on his marathon race stepping on the fertile soil of the village barefooted, and still running towards the same route that leads to the palace, before he bumped into someone as soon as he turned his back; not as if he's being chased by anyone).

PALACE GUARD: What have you done you stupid boy? You just knocked the prince of this village off his feet. Are you dumb, don't you have manners?

UDO: I'm sorry my prince, I got distracted while sprinting.

PRINCE: Stand back, guard! What's your name?

UDO: My name is Udo, and please are you the prince?

PALACE GUARD: You don't respond to a question of the prince, with your own question; you're simply a peasant.

PRINCE: Guard, I clearly told you to stand back!

PALACE GUARD: Please forgive my manners, your highness.

PRINCE: You said Udo, right?

UDO: Yes your highness, that's my name.

PRINCE. Why were you running like someone has put a price on your head, or did you steal?

(Udo became speechless and clueless)

PRINCE. I see you're a very shy guy; which is strange, because I'm yet to see one in this village. All the men I've come across are mostly so bold, fearless and brave. You also look so handsome for a man, and you're light-skinned, which is also rare to see; since the men of this village are mostly dark-skinned. I guess you haven't been in a battle before?

UDO. Not at all, your highness; I'm yet to slay or get slain on the battlefield.

PRINCE. I see, Udo; how about you come with me? I was on my way to the battleground near the marketplace, to watch wrestlers wrestle each other to the ground.

(Udo nods as his approval to the prince's proposal).

PRINCE. You're indeed a shy guy, and although I'm the prince; my hobby is to observe people, and everything about them including their behavior and any weird act of them. Udo, I must say you captured my attention as soon as I saw you, which makes me more interested in getting to know you.

PALACE GUARD. My prince, don't you think it's too generous of you to be so comforting with a stranger you know nothing about? Though, I recognized him as a member of this village.

PRINCE. You see why I was reluctant to step out of the palace with any guard; y'all find it so difficult not to speak when you're asked to stay silent.

**PALACE GUARD.**  Please forgive me once again, your highness; I'll mind my
business from now on.

**PRINCE.**  That's the way it should be! Udo, join me in front, let both guards
follow at the back.

## ACT 5, SCENE TEN

**ULOMA.**  Where are you coming from by this time of the night?

**UDO.**  Nne m, this one you're sitting outside; have you been waiting for me?

**ULOMA.**  Udo, you ran away from home since morning, right in the middle of
your discussion with papa. Do you expect me to happily and

unworriedly go to bed without knowing the whereabouts of my only child?

**UDO:** Nne m, I'm so sorry about my actions in the presence of Nna anyi.

**ULOMA:** Udo, where are you coming from?

**UDO:** Nne m, agara m ile mgba (it means; I went to watch wrestling, in the lingo used).

**ULOMA:** Udo, this time you didn't go to the palace, but now to the market square, to watch muscular men wrestle. The gods of our land; why does this child want to lead me to my early grave, same fate as his father's.

**UDO:** But Nne m, I didn't go alone; the prince asked me to accompany him over there.

**ULOMA:** Udo, are you sure you don't have a loose screw?

**UDO:** Nne m, I was shocked as well, but it's the prince in person; he is of average height, dark-skinned, not too thin, and he's good-looking. Lest I forget Nne m, he was putting on Isiagu (traditional attire designed with the head of a lion) and beads; which covered his nudity and exposed his royalty, respectively. But I'm stalked with this loincloth that covers only my private part and still exposes part of my buttocks, each and every single day.

**ULOMA:** Udo, you should never feel ashamed of your way of dressing, for its part of your culture. Take a look at me your mother; I'm always proud of tying my two wrappers, which covers my upper body and waist, separately. Now tell me Udo, what did you follow the prince to do at the wrestling ground?

**UDO:**  Nne m, after I ran out in the middle of my discussion with Nna anyi, I bumped into the prince unknowingly, on his way to the wrestling ground.

**ULOMA:**  You bumped into the prince, Udo; why can't you go a day without causing trouble for yourself, and now it seems you've chosen the royal family as your targets, since you're the terror?

**UDO:**  Nne m, it's not like that, and besides, the prince was so considerate towards me.

**ULOMA:**  Which scares me, Udo; we don't even have any noble background, we are simply commoners. Now tell me; when you followed the prince to the battleground, did you or the prince join them to wrestle?

**UDO:**  I was watching at first, before the prince asked me to come serve the wrestlers, the jar of palm wine, he brought along.

**ULOMA:**  Did no servant accompany the prince?

**UDO:**  He had two guards with him, but he preferred me closer, to them.

**ULOMA:**  Ewuchim oo (she worriedly cried out)! Udo, I do not like this at all; without concealing anything, now tell me in details all the prince asked you to do?

**UDO:**  Nne m, I enjoyed my outing with the prince, I can't lie about that.

**ULOMA:**  Udo, I might not be as hot tempered or as scary as my uncle; who's also like a father to me and like a grandfather to you. But if you don't tell me the details of everything, the prince asked you to do; I'll pluck out your eyes with my bare hands, and maybe it will do you a lot of good not to see at all, than to sexually stare at the nakedness of your fellow man.

**UDO:**  Don't get like that, Nne m; it's not my fault that I can't help but feel sexually attracted to a man, and not a woman.

**ULOMA:**  Udo, may the gods cut off your tongue for spewing such arrant nonsense! What did the prince ask you to do, speak up?

**UDO:**  Nne m, promise me, you won't get angry nor scold me if I tell you?

**ULOMA:**  As far as I can recall, Udo; I've never flogged you since giving birth to you, that's to show you that regardless of my mood swings, I'm also considerate towards you.

**UDO:**  Nne m, the prince also asked me to dance for him, while the wrestling cheerleaders beat the drum.

**ULOMA:**  What again did he ask you to do?

**UDO:**  He gave me his neck beads and told me to place it on my waist, then freely allow myself move like a lady in his presence.

**ULOMA:**  Udo, did the prince come onto you in a seductive way?

**UDO:**  No Nne m, he only told me to shake my buttocks and whine my waist faster.

**ULOMA:**  Did you comply with all the demands of the prince in public?

**UDO:**  Yes Nne m, the people all clapped and even cheered for me.

**ULOMA.**  Udo, I want you to draw your ears so you can clearly hear what I'm going to say!

**UDO.**  Nne m, I'm holding my ears like you asked me to, now please tell me what you want to say.

**ULOMA.**  Udo, after today, I don't want to ever see you in the prince's corner as long as I'm still alive.

**UDO.**  But Nne m, my outing with the prince today, didn't yield any trouble for you to be wary of.

**ULOMA.**  it didn't today, but it probably will, tomorrow! Udo, did you hear what I just said?

**UDO.**  Nne m, I can't promise you, I'm going to stay away from the prince's path.

**ULOMA.**  Udo, since when have you become so gutsy that you'd even talk back at your mother?

**UDO.**  Nne m, at least tell me, why you want me to stay off the prince's path.

**ULOMA.**  Fine Udo, I'll tell you; you are facing insecurities with your sexual orientation, and with what you told me, one could clearly agree that the prince has an ulterior motive, which will most likely bring doom to our family. Do you understand now?

**UDO.**  Yes Nne m, I clearly understand. But Nne m, is it my fault that I can't control my desires to fantasize about muscular men?

**ULOMA.**  Udo, I'm not going to put the blame solely on you, it could also be that, I'm to blame as well. However Udo, I want you to go to bed right

now, seeing how sleepy you are; you keep yawning, which gives you
away.

**UDO:** Please Nne m, can you answer my question?

**ULOMA:** Udo, your sexual desire for men may not be your fault; hopefully, I'll
discover the reason behind your sexual orientation very soon, after my
outing with papa tomorrow, I hope.

**UDO:** Nne m, where are you and Nna anyi going to?

**ULOMA:** Udo, go get some rest; it's also possible I'll be gone before you're
awake. So I can come back on time and prepare abacha and ugba (a
dish also known as African salad in common), for your lunch.

**UDO:** Nne m, you'll prepare my favorite dish for me?

**ULOMA:** I will, Udo, so go get some rest, and you know you haven't recovered
fully from the lashing you endured the other day.

**UDO:** Nne m, ka chifoo (it means; good night, in the lingo used).


## ACT 5, SCENE ELEVEN

### Agadigba Shrine

**DEDE:** Uloma, have you ever been to a shrine in the past?

**ULOMA:** I never even pictured myself visiting one, Dede.

**DEDE.** I see Uloma, however, what comes to your mind when you hear, Agadigba shrine?

**ULOMA.** Dede, to be honest; I see it as a place where rituals for good and bad omen are carried out, and a place which a woman shouldn't dare visit.

**DEDE.** You're right though, especially when you said it isn't a place for women to visit; mostly without a purpose. Some shrines from the neighboring villages forbids the entrance of a woman, however, Agadigba is a shrine that welcomes the presence of everyone who lives in this village, as long as you came for a noble cause; but he's not welcoming to a visitor or foreigner. We came here for a never before experienced matter in this village, which needs a solution, and a solution we shall get. Let's go in, Uloma; and I must caution you not to speak but listen while Agadigba speaks, for he doesn't repeat nor go back on his words.

**ULOMA.** I've heard all you said, Dede, and I'll do all it takes to see that my son is able to use his manhood, like the man he is.

(Agadigba is the name of the shrine; Udo's mother followed her uncle to visit, in other to find a solution for Udo's sexual orientation. The chief priest made his way into the shrine, by walking in with his back; he also wore a red garment, with white powder carving an arc around one of his eyes, and placing a leaf between his lips. He gently removed the leaf from his mouth, and spoke directly to Udo's mom and her uncle).

**EZEMMUO.** what brings you both here?

(Udo's uncle chose himself as the mouthpiece)

**DEDE.** Ezemmuo (it means; chief priest, in the language used), we came here to find out how is it possible for my niece's son, to sexually desire his fellow man.

**EZEMMUO.** (laughing and making incantations to the gods, to also seek if a solution is available, and he did so for some minutes). Listen attentively, I've consulted Agadigba; what you said could result in a bad omen for this village, and now you can feel how heavy the storm has become, which shows the gods are infuriated by what this child in question could cause in this kingdom.

**DEDE.** What is the solution on ground, Ezemmuo?

**EZEMMUO.** That child has to be killed immediately; to eradicate any form of a bad omen befalling this village and the people.

**ULOMA.** Ezemmuo, I rather die, than ever have my one and only child killed!

**DEDE.** Will you shut up, Uloma; I thought I clearly told you not to interrupt Agadigba, while he speaks! Don't you know he speaks through his messenger?

**ULOMA.** Ezemmuo, thanks for nothing, I'll be on my way now.

**EZEMMUO.** Woman, I'll warn you to act now or I'll be forced to act on your behalf later; you gave birth to an evil child, and he must die now, before he brings a catastrophic end to this village.

**ULOMA.** (Udo's mom laid down a threat to the chief priest, with heavy tears rolling down her cheeks); Ezemmuo, if anything should happen to my son, then I'll run as fast as I can to your shrine so you can have me killed as well!

**DEDE.**  Uloma, I said keep shut! Ezemmuo, we shall be on our way now, and please forgive my niece; I'll give your warnings a deep thought, and if need be, I'll kill Udo myself.

**ULOMA.**  Dede, you will do no such thing! I'll never be alive and watch anyone kill my son, except you kill me first, Dede!

**DEDE.**  Uloma, I said you should keep shut!

**ULOMA.**  No I won't, Dede; no one will kill my son! I promise you, I'll save my son no matter what it takes, and I'll also see to it that he regains his manliness.

(Udo's mom couldn't stand the thought of having her own child killed, as she puts her hands on her head, and walked as fast as possible out of the shrine; she cared less about her uncle that brought her to the shrine, as she went and left him behind).

## ACT 6, SCENE TWELVE

**ETEMMA.** Is that not Uloma, that's sitting all alone by the stream? Uloma!
Uloma!! But why is she crying?

(The yet to be identified person approached Udo's mom, who came over to the
stream in the village to cry away her sorrows).

**ETEMMA.** Uloma, where did you keep your ears? I've been calling your name.

**ULOMA.** And who are you; did they send you to kill my son?

**ETEMMA.** Uloma, it's me your childhood friend; Etemma.

ULOMA. Etemma, are you really the one?

ETEMMA. Look at my face now; my beauty hasn't faded in anyway. But
Uloma, why are you crying and saying, "They want to kill your son"?

ULOMA. Because it's the truth, Etemma; Ezemmuo (the chief priest) wants to
have my son, Udo, killed.

ETEMMA. Uloma, may the gods of our land forbid such atrocity! Why will
Ezemmuo want to kill Udo?

ULOMA. I prefer not to tell you, Etemma; I just don't trust anyone anymore, and
the more I feel this issue is exposed, the more fearful I become over the
safety of my son.

ETEMMA. Uloma, we've been friends even before you had your son at just 17
years of age; still, you tell me to my face, that you don't trust me. Is
this how strong our friendship bond has become?

ULOMA. Etemma, there are so many things going through my head right now,
please understand me. However Etemma, when did you get back from
your husband's place?

ETEMMA. Uloma, enwerem akuko ka m gwa gi (it means; I have a story to tell
you, in the lingo used).

ULOMA. Etemma, hope all is well?

ETEMMA. What can I tell you, Uloma; my husband chased me and our only
child out of the house.

ULOMA. But how is that possible, Etemma? Your husband paid your dowry
with cowries, and he also completed the marriage rites that made you
his wife for the past 16 years.

ETEMMA. My dear Uloma; the issue is our daughter, Gollibe.

ULOMA. Really Etemma, so what does your daughter have to do with this?

ETEMMA. Uloma, let's leave the waterway first, before I'll tell you; the water
hides people we can't see or hear, but they can see us and hear us.

(It so happens Etemma is the unidentified person who approached Uloma, and it's
also understood that Etemma is the childhood friend of Udo's mother. But what
could she be trying to tell Uloma, about her daughter, whose name is Gollibe?
Let's find out).


ETEMMA. Uloma, I think here is a good spot to tell you, for there are no walls
around, and you know the walls also have ears, right?

ULOMA. Yes Etemma, please let's skip the suspense and cut to the chase. What
does your daughter, Gollibe, have to do with the end of your marriage?

ETEMMA. Uloma, my daughter seeks sexual pleasure from her gender.

ULOMA. Ala Umu Obodo!

ETEMMA. Uloma, don't call the name of this village now; do you want the
people to come bear witness to my testament? I expect you to keep
this a secret.

**ULOMA:**   Etemma; will you believe me when I tell you that my son is going through this same unseen fate, in the entire existence of Ala Umu Obodo?

**ETEMMA:**   Isi gini (it means, "You say what", in the lingo used)? Uloma, are you trying to tell me that our children are reliving the same fate, in their opposite gender?

**ULOMA:**   My dear friend, how I wish I can tell you otherwise. The strangest thing is even Ezemmuo said it's a bad omen, and he told me, "My son has to be killed". Etemma, can you kill or watch your own daughter get killed?

**ETEMMA:**   Over my dead body; I won't stand and watch my only daughter get killed. To even top it off, Uloma, this was the same thing my husband had proposed, "That we both kill our daughter". Uloma, I rejected such proposal immediately, for it is impossicant and unthinkable, while I'm still alive.

**ULOMA:**   But Etemma, what do you think made our children this way?

**ETEMMA:**   Uloma, I think its genetics, and I believe it's from their genes, and not hereditary. We both agree that this has never being experienced in our lineage; that means it couldn't have been inherited from neither, we the parents, nor, grand and great-grandparents.

**ULOMA:**   Etemma, does that mean, we aren't the actual cause of it?

**ETEMMA:**   Not at all, Uloma; theoretically, I see reasons to support nonsocial and biological causes of sexual orientation, than social ones. This means there is no substantive evidence which suggests parenting or early childhood experiences play a role with regard to sexual orientation.

**ULOMA.**   Etemma, how come you're educated about this topic?

**ETEMMA.**   My dear Uloma, you can't expect me to fold my arms and sit idly by, while my daughter goes through this phase of her life, all alone. I actually inquired the medical opinion of the midwife who helped me conceive my daughter, Gollibe.

**ULOMA.**   I can't believe it, so I can now lessen the guilt on myself, that I'm not the main cause of Udo's sexuality?

**ETEMMA.**   Yes, Uloma; the midwife told me it's a natural variation in human sexuality. And she also told me, she got a summary and idea of this from her late mother, who also experienced this with a patient of hers during her time.

**ULOMA.**   If so Etemma, then there's a solution on how her mother's patient from then, dealt with her child's sexuality?

**ETEMMA.**   I thought so too, Uloma, but she sadly said the patient went into hiding with that child from then, just to protect the child from being condemned to death.

**ULOMA.**   Etemma, we won't stay idle and watch our children die mysteriously, either; so what do you think we should we do?

**ETEMMA.**   For now my friend, we both are clueless and ignorantly floating in the same boat; short of ideas and without a solution.

ULOMA. Etemma, what scares me the most is the prince of this kingdom might try to exploit Udo's sexual desires.

ETEMMA. Uloma, do you mean the royal prince is also involved in this forbidden plot?

ULOMA. I fear so, Etemma; yesterday, he asked my son to dance and move like a courtesan in his presence, and he even went as far as giving, Udo, the royal bead to hang on his waist.

(Both coincidentally spoke at the same time, **"We better act fast"**).


## ACT 6, SCENE THIRTEEN


UDO. Nne m, you told me you'll come back before noon, in other to prepare my favorite dish for lunch, and now you're returning this evening. What took you so long?

ULOMA. Udo, come give me a tight hug; make sure you don't let go.

UDO. Why the sudden show of affection, Nne m?

ULOMA. Just hug me my son, and I promise you no one will take you from me; even if it involves my death.

UDO. You're scaring me, Nne m; what's going on?

ULOMA. Don't speak, my son; I only want to feel your heartbeat with mine.

**UDO:** Nne m, does this have to do with the place, you told me you're going to visit with Nna anyi?

**ULOMA:** I don't want you to bring papa into this, no one will separate you from me, and that's a fact; I'll be your shield, my son.

**UDO:** Nne m, won't you tell me what's going on; why do you speak in riddles?

**ULOMA:** You know what, Udo? I'll go prepare the abacha and ugba (also known as African salad in common), which I promised to prepare for you today.

**UDO:** Nne m, I already ate Ona (local yam) and palm oil.

**ULOMA:** Udo, I don't mind to feed you more and more; as long as you'll remain alive and healthy for me.

**UDO:** Not like I'm going to die anytime soon, Nne m; so why are you so worried?

**ULOMA:** Don't mind me, my son; I love you too much, so it's normal for me to worry even more. However Udo, promise me, you won't leave our hut without seeking my consent first?

**UDO:** Nne m, is anyone planning on having me killed?

**ULOMA:** No my son, I'm only making sure you're safe and well protected. Now come hug me again, before I go and prepare your favorite dish.

(Uloma couldn't control her outpour of love on her son, Udo, after being traumatized by the threat of having him killed for being homosexual; a never before experienced and unseen issue in the village. It is immediately regarded as a bad omen and the death of Udo, is a supposed way of preventing this bad omen from befalling the village).


## ACT 6, SCENE FOURTEEN


### The Next Morning

ULOMA. Who are you and have they sent you to also kill my son?

PRINCE. Please calm down Mama, and I presume you're Udo's mother?

ULOMA. Yes, I am both the father and mother of Udo; I'm also his protector and his defender. In short, go and tell your sender, "Abum Agada Gbachiri Uzo" (it means; I am the roadblock, in the lingo used).

PRINCE. I came here of my own freewill, and I didn't come to hurt anyone, so please refrain from doing anything you'd regret.

ULOMA. Who are you please, because you're yet to state your mission in my hut?

PRINCE. I'm the prince of this kingdom, and I came to see, Udo.

ULOMA. Please forgive my manners, your highness!

PRINCE. No problem, Nne Udo (Udo's mother); is he in?

**ULOMA:**  My prince, to be honest with you; I don't want you to look for my
son anymore. He is all I have, and I don't want him or myself getting
involved in any trouble with the royal family; because of
the supposed friendship of you two.

**PRINCE:**  You have nothing to worry about, Nne Udo; my friendship with Udo,
won't cause any harm for neither him nor you.

**ULOMA:**  My prince, how about I tell you personally that I don't want you to
befriend my son at all?

**PRINCE:**  Nne Udo, but I've assured you I mean no harm to your son, or even,
you; so why are you still not in support of our friendship?

**ULOMA:**  My prince, I know it's forbidden for a commoner like me, to raise my
voice at a member of the royal family; but I'll appreciate if you don't
come looking for my son again, it's as simple as that.

**PRINCE:**  It's all fine, Nne Udo; I'll be taking my leave, but please send my
regards to your son, Udo.

**ULOMA:**  My prince, you can be rest assured that I won't send your regards to
my son; but it will be a pleasure of mine, "To see you take your leave".


## ACT 6, SCENE FIFTEEN


**UDO:**  My prince! My prince!!

**PRINCE.** Oh my; Udo, where did you come from?

**UDO.** I heard your entire conversation with my mother, and I'll like to apologize on her behalf; biko gbaghara nne m (it means; please forgive my mother, in the lingo used).

**PRINCE.** I've already forgotten about it, Udo; but I'm more concerned about how you came outside?

**UDO.** My prince, I knew my mother in the mood she's in right now, won't allow me go through the door, regardless of how I persist; so I opted for the window of my room.

**PRINCE.** Are you for real, Udo, like why did you do that?

**UDO.** For the same reason you came to visit me, your highness.

**PRINCE.** Hmm I see, so what's the reason according to you?

**UDO.** How about you say it first? (Udo showed more of his feminine side when he blushed and smiled).

**PRINCE.** You don't just look handsome, but so beautiful, when you smile, Udo.

**UDO.** My prince, hope you aren't just flirting with me?

**PRINCE.** I'll be straight, Udo; I came to visit you because I missed your presence and I want to feel you more by my side.

**UDO.** I also missed you, my prince; even though we saw each other, a day before yesterday.

**PRINCE.**   Let's not waste time, Udo. Come with me, let's take a walk; I know a
place, you'd like.

**UDO.**   But my prince, I don't know if I should come with you.

**PRINCE.**   Why do you say so?

**UDO.**   My mother's extra show of affection towards me, I've been scaring me;
she even talked like someone is after my life, and she also told me to
promise her not to come close to you again.

**PRINCE.**   I see, she also acted weird when she saw me in your hut, she made
a remark like; was I the one they sent to kill her son? Do you think
something is wrong with her, Udo?

**UDO.**   I truly hope not; because Nne m, is all I have in this world, and I don't
know if I'll be able to move on if something happens to her.

**PRINCE.**   Don't you know I'm also here for you?

**UDO.**   You make me smile, my prince; I hope your sweetness towards me doesn't
turnout becoming a nightmare of mine.

**PRINCE.**   It won't Udo, and I'll tell you this, just so you can be rest assured that
I'll always be available for you; no matter what time of day it is, I want
you to come to the palace and ask of me.

**UDO.**   I'm not sure I can do that, my prince.

**PRINCE.**   But why won't you be able to?

**UDO.**   My prince, I don't think Igwe will like that at all.

**PRINCE:**   What concerns Igwe, who's also my father, with our friendship?

(Udo summarized the panic attack he had because of the lashing, the king ordered his guards to unleash on him, for roaming around the palace premises, and for not showing his balls as a man).

**PRINCE:**   Udo, do you mean my father suspects your femininity?

**UDO:**   Yes, my prince; Igwe already suspects my sexuality, for behaving girlish in his presence. This is why I don't think I'll be able to visit you at the palace; I don't think I'll survive another lashing on my buttocks.

**PRINCE:**   I'm not trying to mock you but this sounds hilarious, Udo; however, my personal quarters is behind the main palace, so you won't have much issues sneaking into my room, if you can promptly enter when the guards that secures my quarters, make their shifts.

**UDO:**   Do you really want me to visit you at the palace, my prince?

**PRINCE:**   I'll be expecting you one of these days, Udo; who knows? We might even spend the night together.

**UDO:**   Do you also like men, my prince?

**PRINCE:**   The first time I met you Udo, I clearly told you; I like observing my environment, which makes me more of a practical person. I've always thought of the idea of deriving sexual pleasure from a man, I want to know how it feels; I'm curious, Udo.

**UDO:**   My prince, do you mean you have a different sexual orientation from mine?

**PRINCE:**   To clear your curiosity, Udo; I've derived sexual pleasures from the maids at the palace, but I couldn't dare with the palace guards, because I know it could cause a catastrophe, if words of such act of mine gets to the ears of Igwe or his cabinet members.

**UDO:**   I feel betrayed, my prince; you simply wanted to use and dump me for your selfish interests. You didn't even care that I have a heart and emotions run deep; just when I thought I could finally fall and feel loved.

**PRINCE:**   It's not entirely true, Udo; I also want to befriend you, you're like the coolest person, I've come across.

**UDO:**   Nne m was right all along, I should have listened to her; you've broken my heart, my prince, and I hope not to ever see nor hear from you ever again.

(Udo runs off yet again, but this time, with heavy tears rolling down his cheeks, seeing how he couldn't take the honest words of the prince, which felt like bullets piercing his heart from every corner).

ACT 7, SCENE SIXTEEN

Seven Days Later

**DEDE.** Onye no n'ulo (it means; who is at home, in the lingo used)? Uloma!

**ULOMA.** Dede, what brings you to my hut?

**DEDE.** Uloma, has it reached the extent of you not ushering me into your hut?

**ULOMA.** Dede, please forgive me and come in.

**DEDE.** Since it has gotten to this, Uloma; I'll prefer to stay outside and state at once what brought me over to your place, not like I came here out of starvation nor to seek shelter. Where is Udo, first off?

**ULOMA.** Dede, my son's whereabouts is none of your concern; please speak so you can leave the same way you came in.

**DEDE.** Its fine, Uloma; have you decided to kill Udo or not?

**ULOMA.** As soon as I heard your voice, Dede; I knew you came here for nothing good. So you've taken it upon yourself to become the

executioner of my own son? Dede, ihere g allme unu nile (it means; you
all shall be put to shame, in the lingo used)!

**DEDE.**   Uloma, I never thought I'll have to tell you this; but you have grains for
brains. Do you think it doesn't break my heart to come to this decision?
Udo has to die for the safety of the people; his sexual desires for his fellow
man will only bring doom to us all and the village at large.

**ULOMA.**   Dede, I also have to tell you this; you sound like a broken record, you
keep spitting dust that cracks your level of wisdom.

**DEDE.**   Uloma, so I now look like your baby boy, you can rain insults on?

**ULOMA.**   Dede, he who wants to be insulted will only speak in a way that will
attract the insults, he deserves.

**DEDE.**   Uloma, if you're not ready to sacrifice your son the easy way, then he
shall be dragged the hard way, to his place of sacrifice. I never make
empty threats, just so you know, Uloma; I'll immediately give Ezemmuo,
**"The go ahead for the sacrifice"**.

**UDO.**   Nna anyi, you want to have me killed?

**ULOMA.**   Udo, go back inside! Who permitted you to come out?

**UDO.**   Nne m, is this why you've tripled and dedicated your affections towards
me? You're scared; Nna anyi will have me killed.

**ULOMA.**   Nobody will kill you, my son! I am your mother and your death shall
be over my dead body. Where are you running to, Udo? Dede,
you've seen what you've caused; I hope you're happy now?

**DEDE.**  Uloma, I never wanted this issue to resort to this.

**ULOMA.**  Dede, Is your conscience judging you now?

**DEDE.**  Keep quiet, Uloma! **"A child that refuses to heed the warnings of the father, will only end up making the same mistakes, the father sounded warnings against"**. The weather is becoming frightening and the thunderstorm is showing signs that this might be the night, **"None of us saw coming"**.

**ULOMA.**  What do you mean, Dede? My son is racing for his life in this rainy night, all because of you, and you're here vomiting leftovers that even the dead won't still feed on. Dede, if either this rain or lightning freezes or strikes my son; I promise you, I'll come back and wash your blood under this rain. Dede, "The desperation of a mother when it comes to protecting her child can never be limited, for she's the one that goes as far as defying an already set limits, and defining her own limits". In this rainy night, my eyes are also pouring out heavily like the rain; but the difference is that my eyes are soaked and pouring out blood, not water. Call all the gods of all the villages to save my son, because if I don't see him as I'm on my way to look for him; then it truly will be, **"The night none of us saw coming"**, like you revealed.

(**"The night none of us saw coming"**; what could truly be behind this rainy and thunderous night in the land of Ala Umu Obodo? So interesting, but let's find out).

## ACT 7, SCENE SEVENTEEN

**PRINCE.** Who is there? Show your face at once! Udo, is that you? Say something; you came here under this stormy weather, heavily drenched. Your eyes are also heavy; I can't even differentiate between, the raindrops from your body and the tears from your eyes. Come close to me, Udo; you look so pale, and traumatized. Did you get hit by the cold hands of a ghost in this rainy night? Please speak up so I can know how to help you, Udo; why did you appear like you resurrected from the dead? Udo, let go of me; why are you embracing me so tightly? Have you suddenly become dumb? Please stop staying mute, Udo. I know all isn't well with you; your warm embrace proves your heart is storing a truckload of worries. Please speak up, Udo; I know you have every right to be livid with me after our last encounter. Udo, I won't lie, my conscience hasn't stopped tormenting me for the past one week; from the day of our last encounter. It also breaks my heart to see you in this condition, Udo; please trust me and let me help uplift the burden that brought you over here. Is anyone after you, or did something happen to your mother?

**UDO.** Nne m!

**PRINCE.** Yes Udo, what happened to your mother?

**UDO.** Nne m, is trying to protect me from Nna anyi.

**PRINCE.** Now I'm completely lost, Udo; who is Nna anyi?

**UDO:**  He wants to kill me!

**PRINCE:**  Udo, you're not making it easy on me, and I don't know how to help you, if you can't speak clearly.

**UDO:**  My prince!

**PRINCE:**  Yes Udo, I'm right by your side; so please tell me who and why they want to kill you?

**UDO:**  Nne m is trying to protect me, but I don't want to die!

**PRINCE:**  Udo, speak in a lower and calmer tone, unless someone might overhear you and try coming in here. Now, take a deep breath and give it another try; who wants to kill you? I'm still confused, Udo.

**UDO:**  Please save me, my prince; I don't want to die.

**PRINCE:**  Udo, I'm getting pissed; how will I save you, if I don't even know who and what I'm saving you from? Udo, I promise to help you. However, first of all tell me who Nna anyi is, and why he wants to kill you, like you claimed?

**UDO:**  He is my mother's uncle, who I also look up to as my grandfather; and now he wants to offer me as a sacrifice.

**PRINCE:**  Your mother's uncle, you don't mean it, Udo?

**UDO:**  I'm very scared right now, my prince.

**PRINCE:**  Then Udo, I guess this is why your mother got so suspicious of someone being sent to kill her son, the last time I visited your hut. You have to remain calm, Udo; no one will hurt you, here in the palace. Take off your wet loincloth, so you won't catch a cold; I'll give you something to change into. Come close to me, so I'll help you untie it, Udo.

UDO. My prince, I'm terrified; my life is in danger.

PRINCE. Udo, do you want me to help you relax, so you can forget all your worries? Stop shaking and come close to me, Udo; I'll make you forget any death threat, you must have heard.

UDO. My prince, how will you help me forget my fears at this point in time?

PRINCE. It's simple, Udo; let my manliness handle your femininity.

UDO. I don't understand, my prince; can you explain better?

PRINCE. Udo, I know you've never experienced sexual pleasure; this night will be your first time, because, that's the only way you'll forget any trauma you're going through currently. Will you allow me take your virginity? I know you can't speak, Udo, and you can't even feel shy; because you're traumatized. However, I can promise you you're going to forget anything at all that bothers you, and you'll come out of your shock; that's the bliss behind sexual fantasy and the purpose of having a good sexual intercourse. Now I'll gently untie your cloths, and I'll turn you on with a passionate kiss, then you'll give in to the magical feeling and come onto me.

(The chief priest promptly appeared in the palace, before the sexual activity of Udo and the prince, began).

**IGWE.**  Ezemmuo (chief priest)! Ogini n'eme (it means; what's going on, in the lingo used?

**EZEMMUO.**  Igwe, the gods are restless!

**IGWE.**  Clear your throat and speak, Ezemmuo; so I can understand you.

**EZEMMUO.**  The gods directed me to appear in the palace, in this ungodly hour; because, as we speak, the prince is involved in a forbidden plot.

**IGWE.**  Ezemmuo, Iwe ne-ewe m (it means; I am getting angry, in the lingo used)! The ways of the gods are not the ways of man, does not imply that the gods will give you an unclear message, which will still remain unclear to the receiver.

**EZEMMUO.**  It's alright Igwe, we shall head for the prince's chamber at once; and then the message, the gods passed to me, will become clearer to you.

**IGWE.**  Then let's not waste any further time, Ezemmuo. Guards! Take the lead and we shall head for the prince's chamber immediately.

**PALACE GUARD.**  Igwe, there's a woman causing a ruckus outside; just so she can forcefully make her way into the palace, unannounced and under the heavy rain.

**EZEMMUO.**  Ha! Ha!! Ha!!! An expected guest has finally arrived; her presence is one I foresaw after leaving my shrine!

**IGWE.**  Why the exasperating laughter, and what do you mean, Ezemmuo?

**EZEMMUO.**  Igwe, order your guards to let her in; what we shall witness in the
prince's room also concerns her.

**IGWE.**  Hmm Ezemmuo, I do not like any of these at all! If there's what I never
tolerate; it is mockery. I am the 14th king of this kingdom, and I've been
on the throne ever since I inherited it from my late father; who died
22years ago. And in my reign, no one have dared ridicule, not to talk of
see me as a laughing stock; don't think it will start now, nor will I tolerate
it from you, Ezemmuo. Guards, let this so-called, "Expected guest", in
immediately!

**PALACE GUARD.**  Here she is, Igwe; woman, pay your respect to the Igwe at
once!

**ULOMA.**  Igwe, pardon my manners, but I didn't come here to see you; I came
over here, because I know my son is here, and my intuition is never
wrong.

**IGWE.**  Who the hell are you, and on what occasion has your wretched son
become a noble guest in my palace?

**ULOMA.**  Igwe, I'm holding my words back because of the crown and Ikenga (it
represents a powerful symbol), in your possession; and please, my son is
not wretched, like you misquoted.

**IGWE.**  Ezemmuo, who the hell is this unbearable woman, you asked me to allow
into my palace? Now I take a closer look, your face is familiar; have I
allowed your presence in my palace, in the past?

**ULOMA.** I am the same woman you forced to watch; how you tried ordering your guards to whip my son to death, not so long ago.

**IGWE.** So you are the proud mother of a forbidden fruit of the womb; a girl child is even more potent, compared to the abnormal child, you birthed.

**ULOMA.** I won't hold back if you curse a child that blessed my womb, and whom I labored tearfully for; I'm just going to forget my respect for you, as the uncaring king of this land.

**IGWE.** Guards, seize her at once!

**ULOMA.** Igwe, and let me tell you this, before your guards seizes me; your own son who's the prince, also suffers from the same abnormality, you claim my Udo suffers from.

**IGWE.** You shall live no more for not knowing how to use your tongue before the Igwe of this kingdom; you pose as a menace in this village and every menace will be eliminated, no matter how perilous. Guards! Behead her at once and leave her body-parts as food for the devourers that perambulate in the jungle.

**EZEMMUO.** Igwe, enwekwaghi oge (it means; there's no more time, in the lingo used)! Let's head to the prince's chamber like we were.

**IGWE.** Is there need for this woman to still be alive, on our way there?

**ULOMA.** Igwe, this concerns her as well. And both of you should brace yourself, for what you're about to see.

**IGWE.**  Let's all go now but you won't escape your death, you this scandalous excuse of a woman! Not even Agadigba will save you; for having a sharp tongue that slices, like a cutlass slaughters.

**EZEMMUO.**  Igwe, tell your guards not to notify the prince; we shall go in like a thief in the night.

**IGWE.**  Ezemmuo, why all this mystery?

**EZEMMUO.**  Open the door and see for yourself, Igwe.

**IGWE.**  I hope this is worth the mystery, and does this lousy woman have to come in as well?

**EZEMMUO.**  You shall take the lead, and we both will follow, and the guards will be the witness.

**IGWE.**  (After seeing the prince and Udo in bed); my eyes have seen what my mouth can't say and even my ears can't hear, not to talk of me believing!

**ULOMA.**  Udo, what have you allowed yourself to commit!

**IGWE.**  Guards, get out immediately!

**EZEMMUO.**  They will go nowhere, Igwe; they will remain as witnesses in place of the council of elders.

**IGWE.**  Ezemuo, i taa m aru (it means; you've bitten me, in the lingo used)! You know this is the forbidden plot, you meant; and you didn't choose to tell me secretly, so as to protect the dignity of the prince, as well as the royal family's. Ekwesiri m iku gi ura, mana i bu mmuo (it means; I'm supposed to slap you, but you're a spirit, in the lingo used)

**EZEMMUO:**  Igwe, onye nwere nwa kwesiri imara otu esi azu nwa ahu (it

means; someone that has a child is supposed to know how to train
the

child, in the lingo used).

**IGWE:**  Woman, you see what this rotten and abnormal son of yours has

blinded my own son to commit; nobody in your family shall be left alive

for this conspiracy against the royal family!

**ULOMA:**  Udo, why did you choose to see me stoned to death with a face of

shame; upon my sacrifices and labor, I've withstood for you, countless

times?

**EZEMMUO:**  Igwe, the message of the gods is now as clear as sunlight to you;

the gods also made it clear that you must not be partial regarding

your judgments in this forbidden plot. What will befall this child

must also befall your son. I shall take my leave, and it will be in

your best interest not to have the blood of this boy's mother on your

hands; because, you are faced with a forbidden plot already. This

could even cause you your throne; which you value in worth of

your own life.

**PRINCE:**  Father, I lack the competence to stare into your eyes; but please, spare

Udo, I took advantage of his state of depression to seduce him.

**IGWE:**  What I saw here, my son; is you being drunk and raped by this bastard,

and this is what everyone that has witnessed this is ordered to say!
You two aren't excluded either; the venomous mother and the forbidden

fruit of hers.

ULOMA.  I will not stoop to your manipulation, Igwe; I thank the gods that your

son the prince, already confessed that he seduced my son who ran from

home after being traumatized by death threats.

IGWE.  Guards! Put this woman and this impotent scoundrel of hers in the cage!

Till I order their temporary release; when I meet and discuss with my

council of elders, regarding she and her son's punishment.

**ACT 8, SCENE EIGHTEEN**

**COUNCIL OF ELDERS.**  Igwe! What is the emergency that made you send

notice for all of us to assemble?

**IGWE:** In my entire reign as the Igwe of this village, I've never felt as ashamed as I feel now to speak before my own council of elders.

**COUNCIL OF ELDERS:** Igwe, but what could dare weigh a strong man like you down in this way?

**IGWE:** I prefer breaking the kolanut as soon as it reaches my hands; I'll go straight to the point. The prince was hypnotized by one riffraff who took advantage of his innocence!

**COUNCIL OF ELDERS:** Igwe, okwu a edobeghi anyi anya (it means; this matter is not still clear to us, in the lingo used).

**IGWE:** The prince was sexually assaulted last night.

**COUNCIL OF ELDERS:** Ahn! Ahn!! Igwe, it is normal for the prince to feel sexually aroused by a damsel; the prince by the way, is ripe for marriage. But who's the girl that dares seduces the prince?

**IGWE:** Elders of our land, if that's the case, I wouldn't have bothered calling y'all, just to inform you.

**COUNCIL OF ELDERS:** Then, what are you yet to tell us, Igwe?

**IGWE:** My son engaged in sexual activity with his fellow man!

(The elders chose to react in native slangs, best used by them; with body movements that weren't unnoticed).

**ONOWU:** Igwe, as the Onowu of this kingdom (second in command after the king); since I've been inducted among the members of cabinet of not only your reign, but also your father's. I've never witnessed or heard this; which I refer to as "Iberiberism".

**COUNCIL OF ELDERS.**  Igwe! Who is this boy in question that involved the prince in this forbidden plot?

**IGWE.**  Guards, fetch him and his insolent mother at once; so they can hear the punishment that befalls them in the presence of the council of elders!

**PALACE GUARD.**  Igwe, here they are.

**DEDE.**  Uloma, m kwuru ya na gi na nwa gi ga-eme ezinulo a ihere (it means; I said it that you and your son will put this family to shame, in the lingo used)!

**ONOWU.**  Chere biko (hold on please); Ichie (a revered title), i maara ndi ha bu (do you know who they are)?

**DEDE.**  Yes, Onowu and my fellow elders; Igwe, I am mortified to tell you that this woman is the daughter of my late sister, and this boy by her side is her only child.

**COUNCIL OF ELDERS.**  Ichie, i si gini (it means; you say what, in the lingo used)?

**DEDE.**  Igwe and my fellow elders; the gods are my witness, when I say I told this woman, she has to kill this child of hers, as Ezemmuo clearly instructed her to do, but still, she refused. And now this son of hers has completely dragged our lineage into the mud! Igwe, I prefer striking while the iron is hot; I won't object if you decide to give this boy the death penalty. But

I beg of you, spare this contemptuous mother of his; so I'll be able to face her mother, when the cold hands of death comes knocking on my door.

**COUNCIL OF ELDERS:**  Igwe, as the council of elders; we see this as an abomination that is yet to be seen nor experienced in this village, even in the era of our forefathers. With this being said, Igwe; the best decision to make will be to uproot the root of this forbidden act at once. And that's to kill this evil boy immediately! Since Ichie here, who's his mother's uncle clearly stated that Ezemmuo saw this as the resolution of the issue at hand. Igwe, gbue ya ozugbo (kill him at once)!

**ULOMA:**  Elders of our land, don't expect me to shine my teeth and applaud y'all, while you try to conspire and have my son killed, just because you won't be the one mourning the loss of your own son; none of you knows the feeling of losing the only fruit of the womb, you're blessed with. I promise y'all, anyone that approaches my son must also have me killed as well, and if you think I'm playing a role as an actress, then I shall prove to you that I mean every word that comes out of my mouth; by showing y'all how naked I was when my late husband impregnated me, and how naked I labored while the midwife helped me conceive this child of mine.

**ONOWU:**  This is a mad woman; nwanyi ara! You have an incurable madness in you! How dare you try to show your nakedness to the Igwe and the elders? This is as big of a slap in the face, as I've seen in my lifetime.

**DEDE.**  Onowu (second in command after the king), please calm down; allow me to reset the brain of this stupid niece of mine.

**IGWE.**  You are incompetent to do so, Ichie! Because if you aren't; your stupid niece like you dubbed her, wouldn't have borrowed your testicles as a man to dare confront me, the king of this kingdom! Their punishment is as follows; I, the Igwe of this kingdom, hereby condemn both mother and son to be faced with decapitation in the forest! I won't accord you the honor of having people watch your disgusting sendoff in the market square. As for you Ichie, I can't keep you anymore as a member of my cabinet, because if I see your face henceforth; I won't be able to forget this forbidden plot orchestrated by descendants of your ancestry. Take them away, guards!

**ULOMA.**  I will pour out my heart with the heavy tears I'm shedding deep down; so I and my son can die together with pride, having in mind that we'll both be received in a more better place, than a village which chooses to punish a commoner, but exonerate the member of a royal family. My son might possess the genes of a female, but the truth is the royal prince took advantage of his lust and weaknesses to sexually abuse him; while Udo, was traumatized by the idea of facing his own death, when he overheard my uncle heartlessly say so.

**PRINCE.**  Elders of our land, I can't remain in my room like my father ordered me to do; just so, I'll remain absolved of my actual actions. I am clearly confessing that I took advantage of Udo's state of shock to derive sexual pleasure from him.

**IGWE:**  Guards, go on with the decapitation without any further delay, and take the prince back to his quarters this instant!

**EZEMMUO:**  Igwe, I clearly passed the message of the gods over to you; that any punishment you decide to befall this woman and her son must also befall the prince, who's as deep in this, as this boy he laid in bed with. You're advised to rethink your decision carefully before you pass on the punishment; except you want to be in a tug of war with the gods of this land that was clearly in existence, long before you and I were born. I shall take my leave, for I'm only the messenger of Agadigba, and I've carried out my mission over here.


## ACT 8, SCENE NINETEEN


### Five Days Later

**COUNCIL OF ELDERS:**  Igwe, the town crier relayed your announcement for everyone in this village to assemble today; it's also five days since you met with us, the council of elders, to decide the best possible way to solve the forbidden plot on ground.

**IGWE:**  I know the entire populace of Ala umu obodo is in attendance, also members of the royal family; the Lolo (Queen), my two princesses and the prince. How I wish this is a special occasion that I invited my people for!

However, it isn't the case; my son who is heir apparent to the throne, has taking it upon himself to perish the long lasting legacy of our royal family. In my 22 years reign as the Igwe of Ala umu obodo, after I succeeded the late king, who was my father, at just 19 years of age; I am yet to see a greater shame than the forbidden plot, my son got involved in, with this rotten boy who kneels in front of me alongside his shameless mother. I don't want to solely put the blame on them, because I don't want the wrath of the gods to befall me or my household. I'm now regrettably admitting to everyone present; the prince had sexual intercourse with this boy who kneels before me. In other words, my son slept with his fellow male counterpart! I am lost for words to defend the actions of the prince; I've rather made my decisions regarding the best way possible to deal with this forbidden plot. This sadly won't be forgotten by the people, neither will it remain untold for generations to come. No matter how it saddens me, I won't make more excuses, instead; I'll man up and face this as the man I am, before the inherited status of a king. Hear my decision and punishment as follows; I hereby banish this boy who is involved in this forbidden plot, together with his mother, they are both banished from this village. On the other hand; I'll abdicate the throne as the 14th Igwe of Ala Umu Obodo, as punishment for the despicable actions and involvement of the prince in this forbidden plot. I and the members of my royal family will also go on exile from this village. In view of the fact that this forbidden plot can never go unwritten in the long existing history of this village; it's in the best interest of the innocent ones, that the roots of this forbidden plot are completely removed from this village. This is why I've decided for both perpetrators together with their families; have to find another life outside their motherland. I honestly wish for this forbidden plot to remain a onetime experience in history, and no such experiences in our dear land again; although, such fate can only be decided by the gods. This is my verdict, for I've spoken my people! I'll never forget the prosperity our land enjoyed, during my reign, all thanks to the sacrifices and hard work of each and every single one of you; thank you, for putting up with the tough times during my reign.

**COUNCIL OF ELDERS.**  Igwe! Igwe i ga-adi!! (This is a show of respect from the elders to the king).

**ONOWU.**  You're also like a son to me, as the dearest friend of your late father, the former Igwe; who I hustled and bustled with during our time. Igwe, your reign shall never be forgotten! You did your best to be a benevolent king, just like your father and grandfather, in short, your predecessors; the people will never forget.

**IGWE.**  Ezemmuo, I have made my decisions known to the people.

**EZEMMUO.**  You did well, Igwe; you showed the impartiality and wisdom, which made the gods believe you were always the right choice, after your father.

**THE PEOPLE.**  Igwe, we all wished things would have turned out differently; so you can rule till your time comes for you to go join your ancestors. However, we'll regard this forbidden plot as the fate, the gods have decided to pass down to this village; traditionally, it hasn't been seen nor heard that a man had sexual intercourse with his fellow man. We shall not talk only about this forbidden plot that transpired during your reign, but we also see reasons to talk about your benevolence in general. Though, you aren't exempted of wrongdoings, but history won't be so unfair to completely condemn your entire reign because of this forbidden plot. Go with the gods, in any place you settle, to call home again.

ACT 9, SCENE TWENTY

**UDO:**  Nne m, biko gbaghara m (it means; please forgive me, in the lingo used).

**ULOMA:**  Udo, thank the gods that you are still alive; I'm your mother and I've never for once judged you, instead I prefer to make your pain, my own pain as well. I don't care if we don't have any place to go from here; I remain grateful to the gods that you are still alive and even by my side. Though we might not have eaten in the last six days, we'll still survive because we have each other; I don't mind building myself a mansion in the evil forest, as far as you're with me, we'll push through and overcome all obstacles. Place your hand on mine, Udo, and let's keep working for there's always a way at the front; as far as we don't turn back.

UDO.   Nne m, I promise to do everything I can so I'll be as manly, as you want me to be; so I'll be able to protect you, like you protected me from birth, and also give you grandchildren to see to it that you reap the fruits of your labor, just like you deserve.

ULOMA.   Don't worry, Udo; I won't rush nor pressure you, but I'll stand by your side every step of the way.

UDO.   Where are we going to spend the night, Nne m?

ULOMA.   Udo, let's keep walking until our legs lack the strength to move any longer; then that will be a place to dwell for the night.

UDO.   And Nne m, if your legs gets so worn-out, mine will still be so lively to even carry you on my back, like you carried me on yours as an infant.

(Udo and his mother, Uloma, were stranded after being banished from the village they both grew in; they had no place to go, and even no belongings to carry from the hut they stayed in. They kept walking and heading for nowhere, before they heard screams).

ETEMMA.   Uloma! Uloma!!

UDO.   Nne m, it seems someone is calling your name.

ULOMA.   Don't look back, Udo, you never could tell if it's a ghost.

UDO.   Do you think we've walked into the land of the dead, Nne m?

**ULOMA.**  It is best you reserve your energy for asking questions as the dinner you'll most likely consume this night.

**ETEMMA.**  Uloma, it's me, Etemma!

**ULOMA.**  Udo, did you just hear, Etemma? That coincides with the name of my childhood friend; on the count of three, let's turn around and confirm if there's a mistaken identity. One! Two! Three! She's recognizably and undeniably the same person, Udo.

**UDO.**  Are you for real; but where could they be heading?

**ULOMA.**  Let's hear from them, Udo.

**ETEMMA.**  Uloma, I've been calling your name since ages ago; why didn't you answer or even look back?

**ULOMA.**  My dear Etemma, it's best to be safe than sorry; you can't expect me to randomly answer any voice that calls my name, when I don't know if it's a stranger or ghost calling. But where are you heading, Etemma, and this must be your daughter by your side?

**ETEMMA.**  Uloma, a great tree has fallen; a messenger came to my father's house this morning, to notify me that, "My husband and father of my daughter is no more".

**ULOMA.**  Oh gods of our land; why does bad things befall good people?

**ETEMMA.**  My dear Uloma, if you ask this question; who do we expect to answer.

ULOMA.  So, Etemma; does this mean you're on your way to your husband's place, who happens to be late now?

ETEMMA.  Yes Uloma, my daughter and I have to go back to oversee the burial and still stay over there; since my late husband is the only child of his late parents. If I may, Uloma; but where are you heading, and I guess this your son, Udo?

ULOMA.  Etemma, my dear friend; this is my son Udo, but the story behind where we are headed is a long and abominable tale, to narrate. But to make the story short; I and my son have been banished, with no place to call home again, and to now make matters worse, we are headed for nowhere. We are simply stranded, my dear friend.

ETEMMA.  You don't mean it, Uloma? Now I recall, does this your case concern the announcement that the town crier made four days ago for every living soul in the village to assemble; based on Igwe's important notice, he wishes to pass across. I even prepared to go to the palace, before the messenger who came from my husband's hometown, notified me of his sad passing.

ULOMA.  My dear Etemma, the case has been judged, and the verdict has been passed; the case is now closed, so I don't wish to reopen it in the middle of nowhere. We've also moved on.

ETEMMA.  Uloma, what do you say if I offer you shelter in my husband's humble abode?

UDO.  Nne m, anything you settle for is also fine with me; whether we go their way, or we go in no direction of ours.

**ETEMMA.** Uloma, it's good to see the bond you share with your son, Udo.

**ULOMA.** Etemma, I have an intuition that the gods sent you to lead us in the right direction; if so, I and my son will also travel with you and your daughter. My daughter, your mom did tell me you're beautiful, but believe me when I say she did you no justice. However, your mom also told me your name, but with so many things on my mind, it seems I can't recall; do you mind reminding me once again?

**GOLLIBE.** Nne Udo; my late father named me, "Gollibe".

**ETEMMA.** There's no time, let's head for my husband's hometown before nightfall.

**ULOMA.** Udo, do you mind assisting Gollibe, with their baggage?

**UDO.** I don't mind becoming their carrier, Nne m.


## ACT 9, SCENE TWENTY-ONE


**GOLLIBE.** You've been standing over there, staring at me all through; won't you step forward, so we can at least play together?

**UDO.** What's the name of this game? I saw how you've been digging holes on the ground and filling it with round stones.

**GOLLIBE.** The name of this game is I'tche; (it is also known as Awele in common). Don't tell me you've never played it before, except you skipped childhood, and impossibly attained adulthood?

**UDO.** It's actually the most preferred hobby of Nne m; though, I've paid little or less attention to it.

**GOLLIBE.** I see, Udo; so what was the most fun memory of your childhood?

**UDO.** You're Gollibe, right?

**GOLLIBE.** Yes Udo, not like you didn't know nor overhear my name being called countless times; now, answer the question I asked you.

**UDO.** Well, the most fun memory of my childhood is playing around with my friend, Nnamdi; we picked sticks and used it to direct and run after wheels we set in motion, all around our village. We also danced and played in the mud while it rains, just to mention a few.

**GOLLIBE.** That sounds cool, Udo. Is it true you like men?

**UDO.** Gollibe, I rather not talk about it, besides, I also knew you like women, but I didn't bother asking you, neither did I make you feel uncomfortable.

**GOLLIBE.** I see you also did a background check, Udo, but tell me; did you roll in the hay with your friend, Nnamdi?

**UDO.** I might have developed sexual desires for men, like myself; however, that doesn't imply, I slept with all my fellow male counterparts that stepped in my path. Also, how did you come to know that I'm homosexual?

**GOLLIBE.** My mother used you as a reference when she tried talking me out of sexually desiring my fellow girls. Now it's your turn, how did you also discover my sexual orientation, Udo?

**UDO.** I saw how you've been staring at Nne m, and behaving around her; it's obvious you have no fear at all when it comes to seeking sexual pleasures, regardless of who it happens to be, Gollibe.

**GOLLIBE.** To be honest, I haven't been able to control my urge for sex whenever they arouse; this is why I've been able to sexually exploit my two female besties, Nenebe and Nkiruka.

**UDO.** You mean you've derived sexual pleasures from your two best friends; Nenebe and Nkiruka?

**GOLLIBE.** That's correct; this is why I've also lost their friendship, since their parent found out. Nevertheless, it has to be known that their sexual orientation still remain unchanged. How about you, Udo; how many sex slaves, have you enslaved?

**UDO.** How ironic, Gollibe; will you now believe me when I tell you that my first time felt like I was the one enslaved; it's simply because I was coerced into it. I won't lie as well, when it comes to fantasizing about sexual encounters with men, that didn't become a reality; then I've sexually fantasized about so many, though, my body count still remains one, and that was a week ago. One week ago, was my first time of having sexual intercourse and that was with the prince of the kingdom, we were banished from.

**GOLLIBE.**  Hmm, that's a tall order, but how did you accomplish that?

**UDO.**  I've admired the prince from the first day, I saw him, and I thought he felt the same way; in reality, he never felt the way I did, he just liked me in his own way.

**GOLLIBE.**  If so, Udo; how did he enslave you to have sex, like you claimed?

**UDO.**  He did by capitalizing on my trauma, to lure and talk me into having sex with him; at a point when I was barely conscious to be held accountable for my actions. On the other hand, the prince is more of a practical person; he only wanted to experience how it felt, to derive sexual pleasures from his fellow man, even when womanizing in the process.

**GOLLIBE.**  Then, you allowed yourself get used and dumped, Udo; didn't it affect your emotions?

**UDO.**  When I found out about the prince's intentions; it broke my heart, but the night I spent with the prince, happened only as a result of the fear of facing my own death, "That was the cause of the trauma, I faced".

**GOLLIBE.**  You've been through a lot, Udo; but do you wish, you were born with a different sexual orientation?

**UDO.**  Sincerely Gollibe; I really didn't care about my sexual preference at first, but having witnessed the tears and torture my mother has endured because of my sexual orientation, it touched and moved me deeply, to the point that I wish I could act more manly. How about you, Gollibe; do you wish you have a different sexual orientation?

GOLLIBE:   I'll be honest, Udo; it's true that I've derived sexual pleasures from
my gender. But still; I don't feel like I lack sexual pleasures nor feel
unsatisfied from the *sexcapades,* I've been on. Udo,
it's my turn to ask; have you wished to seek sexual pleasures from a
woman?

UDO:   It hasn't crossed my mind for once; I keep asking myself why I feel turnoff
from the opposite gender. Have you thought of seeking pleasures from a
man, Gollibe?

GOLLIBE:   I've thought of the possibility, not once but twice; it's just that I'm
yet to see a man who's available. Who knows maybe I'll sneak into
your mat at night, one of these days and engage in sexual activity with
you, "Just so I'll know how it feels like to have sexual intercourse with
a man". I see you're a shy guy, you can't even laugh out loud, you
prefer to smile sheepishly and hide your fine face; well, I was just
kidding, Udo. Sit down so we can both play and enjoy the I'tche (a
game commonly known as, "Awele").


(It so happens that Etemma, who is Gollibe's mom, was close by while the
conversation of Udo and Gollibe was ongoing, also Udo's mom, Uloma, saw it all)

ETEMMA:   Uloma, are you seeing what I'm seeing?

ULOMA:   I'm hugely interested in what I'm seeing, my dear Etemma.

ETEMMA:   Who could have envisioned your son, Udo, and my daughter,
Gollibe, bonding like they've known each other from way back?

On second thought, Uloma; could this be a sign or an indirect vision
we are still yet to grasp?

ULOMA:   Now you brought this to my knowledge, Etemma; I agree, and it
shows we collectively share the same thought right now. (They both
shared their opinion at the same time, "How about we plan so my child
can spend the night with your child? I guess we shared the same
thought
after all"). Now we've both said it, Etemma; how can we get them both
to spend the night?

ETEMMA:   Come to think of it, Uloma; let's get them intoxicated, and there's a
charm I can obtain, that'd make them hypnotized as well. In other
words, they'll fail to recognize themselves at that point in time; more
like act without their senses for some minutes.

ULOMA:   Etemma, how sure can we be that they'd make love to each other?

ETEMMA:   The charm I'm talking about will also boost their sexual organs, and
enhance their horniness.

ULOMA:   What you just said, sounds too good to be true, Etemma; where will
you get such charm from?

ETEMMA:   Like I said earlier, obtaining the charm won't be an issue; I can
obtain it from the midwife who helped me conceive Gollibe. The same
midwife gave me that charm, to heighten my chances of
childbearing; since it took me time to get pregnant after four years of
marriage.

ULOMA: If so, Etemma; you have my consent to carry on with the plan. However, let's give them at least seven days to see if they'll do it willingly with each other, and also, so they can feel relaxed and rest more; since we've only arrived here, three days ago. The question still remains; how sure are we that this will help change their sexual orientation?

ETEMMA: That question will best be left for the gods to answer; for now, we can only do our part and leave the rest to our hope and believe.

## ACT 9, SCENE TWENTY–TWO

### A Week Later

ULOMA: What took you so long and hope you were able to give her some cowries and collect the charm?

ETEMMA: Come on Uloma, you should know me by now that I don't return from an errand, except I've gotten what I actually went for.

ULOMA: My bad, you're right Etemma; but where's the charm?

ETEMMA: It's in between my breast. But before we carry on; where's Udo and Gollibe?

ULOMA: I see you've also forgotten that I've always being good, when it comes to convincing people; I did convince Udo and Gollibe to go fetch water from the stream, just so they won't be available while we carry out our hidden agenda.

**ETEMMA:**  You did well, Uloma; but I still wonder while Udo and Gollibe didn't think it through to derive sexual pleasure, even after the pair has found chemistry between them.

**ULOMA:**  Well, my dearest Etemma, we've waited while we could; now it's simply time to act and save our children's future. Lest I forget, Etemma; where exactly, are we going to put the charm?

**ETEMMA:**  I also bought a jar of palm wine on my way back from the midwife's home.

**ULOMA:**  I must recommend your thoughtfulness, Etemma; however, we have to be extremely careful not to get them too intoxicated, that they could totally lose consciousness.

**ETEMMA:**  I've thought of that, Uloma, and that's why I decided we offer them not more than two cups of the palm wine. Also, the charm will immediately become effective once I pour and shake it in the jar of the palm wine.

**ULOMA:**  Hold on, Etemma; will you pour all the portion of the charm?

**ETEMMA:**  It's going to be half of the portion; because the midwife cautioned me on the effectiveness, it possesses. The effect will boost their sexual organs, and with the mixture of the alcohol in the palm wine; it will make them lose concentration of their reality, and they most likely will act out of their senses.

**ULOMA.** My dear friend; we can only hope this works, let's hold on till night
before giving them to drink, so exhaustion from the day's task, will also
have its effect.

**ETEMMA.** I support your view, Uloma; how about they ask what we are
celebrating, since we want them to drink palm wine, which is mostly
preserved and enjoyed for special occasions?

**ULOMA.** Come to think of it, Etemma; today is the 4th of the current month,
right?

**ETEMMA.** Yes, Uloma; today is the 4th of the second month of the year. But is
there anything special about today, Uloma?

**ULOMA.** It's not a special occasion, now I clearly remember; it tallies
with the same date, I lost my late husband, who's also Udo's father.
On that very day, he went hunting for bush meat, after he promised to
treat me to a special delicacy that night; sadly did I know he will end
up becoming the delicacy for wild animals. He was a hunter that went
hunting, and became the hunted.

**ETEMMA.** Uloma, this shows the gods is truly in our favor; once you
emotionally tell this to Udo, he definitely will want to pay his respect
once again, and it will indeed be a good reason for him to have a
drink, in honor of his father's memory.

**ULOMA.** How about your daughter, Gollibe; do you think she'll be willing to
help *pleasurize* Udo, after they both would have drank out of the jar of
palm wine?

**ETEMMA:** I'd say, "Yes"; my daughter is very sensual, her urge for pleasure is insatiable. She's one who wishes to give in to the desire once her honeypot gets turned on; she has even gone as far as trying to molest me, her own mother.

**ULOMA:** What! Gollibe has gone that far; is she that fearless?

**ETEMMA:** She took after the fearlessness of her father; from his childhood till his adulthood, he never backed down from standing toe to toe with anybody that has tried getting in a combat with him, or also tried using words to make him feel threatened.

**ULOMA:** Then, how did you get her under control, when she tried molesting you?

**ETEMMA:** Just like I said she inherited the fearlessness of her father, also, she inherited the compassion of her mother; that's why when I reason with her deeply, she regains her senses, and consequently apologizes. Though I must say; this happened only twice, and hopefully, not again. Funnily enough, she can't match me for strength, even if my words can't get her tamed.

**ULOMA:** Oh my, they are already back; let's leave the gist and play along.

**ETEMMA:** Welcome back my lovely children!

**ULOMA:** Hope you fetched the water?

**UDO:** Nne m, we fetched the water, but we got delayed because; Gollibe talked me into playing with some of her friends, we came across at the stream.

**ULOMA.**  It's all fine, Udo; now say your greetings to Gollibe's mother.

**UDO.**  Nne Gollibe, ekene m gi (it means; I greet you, in the lingo used).

**ETEMMA.**  May the gods bless you, my son. I'm also glad Gollibe is showing
you around the village; I know adapting to a new environment isn't
easy.

**GOLLIBE.**  I've been doing my best to help Udo settle in our small village,
mama.

**ETEMMA.**  You've done excellently well so far, Gollibe, and as your mother,
I'm super proud of you, my daughter.

**ULOMA.**  Now, you two should go pour the water, you've fetched into the clay
pot in the kitchen, and carry your covered foods as well.

**UDO.**  Thank you, Nne m; it seems you knew we are both famished. Take the
lead, Gollibe, I'll be right behind.

**GOLLIBE.**  As you wish, Udo, but you have to assist me in putting down this pot
of water on my head.

(Due to the setting of the story, which followed the setting of ancient days; clay
pot was used to fetch and store water for different purposes, rather than kegs and
storage cans, which are available in modern era).



## ACT 9, SCENE TWENTY-THREE

ETEMMA.   It's nighttime; so let's act like we agreed, Uloma. I'll go in and
        bring Gollibe, while you go remind Udo that today is his father's
        remembrance. We'll meet up with you in the middle of your
        conversation with your son.

ULOMA.   I'm on my way Etemma, but I'm still wondering; what if tonight
        doesn't yield our desired result?

ETEMMA.   It's simple, Uloma; then we'll repeat this act tomorrow,
        next tomorrow, and the days after; we won't back down till we
        achieve our desired purpose

ULOMA.   I believe our efforts won't be in vain, Etemma; we can't doubt the
        process or lose hope now.

ETEMMA.   Get going, Uloma; Udo is singing under the tree.

(Uloma approached Udo, just as her childhood friend, Etemma, directed her)

ULOMA.   Udo!

UDO.   Yes Nne m, can I be of help?

ULOMA.   Come closer, Udo; I have something to tell you.

UDO.   Here I am, Nne m; you interrupted the melodious tone, I sang out to the
        birds.

ULOMA.   Udo, I don't know how to say this, but you still have to know about it.

**UDO:**  Nne m, is there still more misery for our broken hearts to still endure? You're crying, Nne m; please don't give me a scare that will put me in a state of shock yet again.

**ULOMA:**  Udo; on this day 18years ago, your father left this world for a better place, just when you were still a newborn.

**UDO:**  Nne m, till now, it breaks my heart that I didn't get to spend more time with my father, and get to experience that fatherly touch and tenderness. The worst part is I even lack description to draw an identical portrait of neither my father's facial features nor body posture. However Nne m, I don't want you to shed any more tear; just like you reiterated, my father is resting in a more better place than earth, which is most likely in paradise.

**ULOMA:**  Udo, as the only son of your father; it's expected of you to drink a cup of palm wine from this jar of palm wine, I brought with me. This cup of palm wine, you're about to drink now; you have to pour some quantity on the floor, as a respect to your forefathers, before you drink the remaining quantity in your father's memory.

**UDO:**  Give me a cup of the palm wine, so I can share with my ancestors and drink in memory of my father's remembrance, like you hinted.

(Gollibe interrupted them, just like her mom had planned).

**GOLLIBE:**  What's going on here?

**ULOMA:**  Don't interrupt Udo, instead you should take a seat, Golibe; today is the remembrance of Udo's father's untimely demise.

GOLLIBE.   I'm so sorry for interrupting; no one told me today's actually your
dad's remembrance, Udo. My mom just came to tell me there's palm
wine outside, incase, I was craving for some, and we all know it's not
every day; we get to drink palm wine. So now it's clear to me that the
special occasion that made the palm wine available is, **"In honor of
Udo's father"**.

ULOMA.   How is the taste of the palm wine, Udo?

UDO.   Nne m, it tastes like a fresh breath of life; I feel my father has now given
me the strength to keep living, so I can continue from where he stopped.
Will you pour me another cup, Nne m?

ULOMA.   Of course Udo, it will be my pleasure to serve you another cup.

ETEMMA.   Gollibe, how about you raise your cup, so I can pour your own drink,
and you'll cheers with Udo?

ULOMA.   Yes, Etemma is right; how about you two cheers to your new found
friendship?

GOLLIBE.   Here is my cup; pour my portion, so I can become Udo's drinking
partner, at least for tonight. But won't our mothers join us?

ETEMMA.   I can't drink for now, Gollibe; we are still in mourning over the
death of your father. So is Uloma; she has to still remain teary, since
today is her late husband's remembrance of his painful exit.

UDO.   But Nne m; why did you allow me to drink? I should also be mourning my
father and not drinking in his honor.

**ULOMA.**  Udo, you completed his remembrance rites by drinking in his honor, which is very important; a child is not supposed to mourn the same way, his mother does.

**ETEMMA.**  Same applies to you, Gollibe; it's a week, your father passed away, so you did the right thing by drinking in his memory.

**UDO.**  Nne m, I'm feeling dizzy and my private part is itching.

**ULOMA.**  What do you expect, Udo? You've finished 3cups without dropping the cup; that will be all, go inside so you can lie down. How about you Gollibe? You've finished 2cups, so it will be wise of you to drop your cup and accompany Udo inside.

**GOLLIBE.**  I want you to accompany me to bed, Nne Udo.

**ETEMMA.**  (She whispers to Uloma); it seems the charm is already having its effects on them. Let's assist them into the room and we'll lock the door, once they lie down, and they'll be left alone in darkness.

**ULOMA.**  Will you give me your hand, Udo; so I can assist you to stand straight?

**UDO.**  Nne m, I don't think you alone can take me to bed. How about you look for a muscular man?

**ULOMA.**  That won't be possible; I've acted as both your father and mother till now, so I can singlehandedly take you in to lie-down.

**GOLLIBE.**  Mama, I want to urinate, I'm so pressed.

**ETEMMA.**  Gollibe, give me your hand, so I can walk you to ease yourself.

(Both Uloma and Etemma took on the task of taking Udo and Gollibe into the same dark room, after intoxicating them with palm wine, and a mix of native charms that makes one tipsy and horny).

**ETEMMA:**  Uloma, why do you still make that face? We've assisted them inside, that means we've completed our task, it's up to them now. Why do you look so disheartened?

**ULOMA:**  To be honest, Etemma; we both know the means we've resorted to, it's not a good one. Udo is only 18 years old, and Gollibe is 16years of age; and here we are exposing them to what I refer as, "Sexual captivity". We are supporting our own children to have unprotected sex; which most likely would lead to more consequences. For instance, Golibe could face early pregnancy at her age, and even worst, they could see this as an opportunity to leave an irresponsible or reckless life; which could turn them into sex slaves. How will we face our late husbands, their fathers?

**ETEMMA:**  I know, right? Uloma, it breaks my heart as well, but a sacrifice must be made for the greater good. You can't expect us to sit idly by and watch our children grow in a way that shame will never depart from each of our lineage. It will be worst when we face our late husbands, and tell them that their child couldn't continue the existence of the family name, by having children of their own to carry on from where they left off; just because they settled and committed their sexuality to the same gender. Uloma, you agreed to this because you want your baby boy to sexually perform like his fellow men, while, I also want

my baby girl to settle down and have a family of hers.

ULOMA.  That's true; you spoke thoughtfully, and I agree with the

sense you made. Etemma, are you with me, why are you going close to

the widow?

ETEMMA.  Uloma, come close, so you can put your ears near the door. What

sound can you hear?

ULOMA.  Etemma, this is really happening; I can clearly hear moans.

Does this mean …?

ETEMMA.  Yes, my dear Uloma; the plan is a success, now we have to wait and

see if the expectation behind this, is finally realized.

ULOMA.  Our hope will never die, my dear friend!


## ACT 9, SCENE TWENTY–FOUR


### The Next Morning

UDO.  What happened last night? It's definitely another creation story; because I

feel like I've been recreated, totally different from the way I felt yesterday.

GOLLIBE.  What do you mean, Udo?

**UDO.**  It's just like I dropped a huge burden off my shoulders; I feel so free
and more comfortable around myself. How about you, Golibe; how do you
feel?

**GOLLIBE.**  If I'm honest; is like I gained a huge satisfaction, after
experiencing a manly touch around my whole body, for the first time.
It's an entirely different feeling from what I'm used to. Udo, what
really happened last night?

**UDO.**  it comes and goes in my head, but I'm yet to clearly visualize last night's
scenario.

**GOLLIBE.**  Udo, could it be we …?

**UDO.**  Gollibe, do you think that really happened?

**GOLLIBE.**  Take a look at yourself, Udo!

**UDO,**  Gollibe! Can you also take a look at yourself?

**GOLLIBE.**  We are naked!

**UDO.**  It's true then; we had sex last night. Gollibe, what have we done?

**GOLLIBE.**  I'm speechless, Udo.

**UDO.**  So am I, Gollibe; what do we do now?

**GOLLIBE.**  Come to think of it, Udo; how about we repeat last night's act?

**UDO.**  Come of it, Gollibe; let's quickly cover our body before your mother or
mine, walks in. However, we have to talk about the feeling, we experienced,

last night. I also want to relieve it, but I don't wish to get into any trouble again.

GOLLIBE. Stop being so scared, Udo; it's time you come out of your mom's wrappers. On a sincere note, we undeniably felt the excitement and a magical touch after deriving sexual pleasure from each other, last night.

UDO. I know, right? I feel like a newborn, or better yet, I found a missing part of my self. It's just like a dream; I even want to go on another *sexcapade* with you, all over again.

GOLLIBE. Udo; I thought I've had all the sexual satisfaction, there is, from the girls I've been with, or even through autoeroticism, but this particular feeling feels like, **"The real deal"**.

UDO. Nne m will be overwhelmed to hear this; she will once again see me, like the male child, she truly gave birth to. Your mother as well, Gollibe; she will have a reason once more to celebrate you, as if she gave birth to you all over again.

GOLLIBE. Udo, before we share the good news with them; let's continue from where we left off last night.

UDO. Get over here, Gollibe; let's see once and for all, if this burning desire truly exists, or a fairytale, too good to be true.

**ACT 10, SCENE TWENTY-FIVE**

<u>Years Later</u>

**ULOMA:**  Udo, I see you've made up your mind and there's absolutely nothing I can do to change your decision. All I'm asking of you now; is for you to take good care of yourself and your family.

UDO: Nne m, be rest assured that I'll sacrifice my life to safeguard my beautiful wife and our three boys.

ETEMMA: Udo, I'll come in here; I've always welcomed you like the son, I never had, even before you tied the knot with my only daughter, Gollibe. Your marriage with Gollibe, have been blessed with three handsome boys, that were all conceived in the last seven years; you two gave we your mothers, the best and biggest gifts, life has to offer. Now you've decided to go back to the village you were born and banished from, though, for a casual visit. Nonetheless, Udo; why have you decided to take your family to visit Ala Umu Obodo?

UDO: First of all; no matter where a man settles for as his dwelling place, he will never find the comfort he felt back at his home. If I don't go back to the place where I was born, and the place where my forefathers called their home; then, I'll have no face to stare at them, when I depart from this world. After I received the messenger, who came here three days ago; I knew I couldn't turn down the opportunity of going back to the route that leads me home.

ULOMA: If I may ask, Udo; what did the messenger want with you?

UDO: Nne m, the messenger had a message from Igwe for me; who requested that I visit him in the palace, in the next three days, and today is the third day.

ETEMMA: Udo, but what could Igwe want to discuss with you; is he not aware that his predecessor banished you for the past 7years?

**UDO.**  I have no idea for now, but once I visit like the Igwe requests, then I shall have answers to your question.

**ULOMA.**  Gollibe, my daughter; please take good care of your husband and your children, y'all should go and come back safely.

**GOLLIBE.**  I'll take your words to heart, mama; you need not worry, for I'll singlehandedly care and cater for my family.

**ULOMA.**  Udo, you have our blessings; go and find out why the Igwe summons you, and please comeback with your family, the same way you left, in one piece.

**UDO.**  Also Nne m, I decided to take my family with me, because, this is the best timing to show everyone in the village; that I might have been mocked and condemned for behaving and possessing the genes of a female, when I resided in my homeland. But now I shall return as the man I am, and a man that's even strong enough to defeat the strongest warrior in the village.

**GOLLIBE.**  We shall be on our way; please, will my mother give us her blessings?

**ETEMMA.**  Of course, though, Uloma's blessing was on my behalf as well, but I'll also give you mine. My son and daughter; may the gods lead y'all to your destination and oversee your protection.

**UDO.**  Ise (Iseee)! (It means, "Let it be so", in the lingo used).

(Udo left with his family immediately, leaving his mom and Gollibe's mom behind)

**ETEMMA.**  Who could have thought this day would come?

**ULOMA.**  Etemma, I've never lacked believe that good things come to people, who have it in themselves to remain patient and hopeful. My son Udo, made the declaration with his own mouth that, **"He is now a Man"**.

**ETEMMA.**  I'm also over the moon, that my daughter is now, **"A Happy Mother"**. At a time, I feared my daughter will deprive herself the right to experience motherhood. At the end of the day, Uloma; we have to be proud for taking it upon ourselves, regardless of all the odds and people against us, to see to it that our children regains their normalcy and potency, in life. Gollibe my daughter, became pregnant a fortnight later; after the day we planned for she and Udo, who's now her husband, to spend the night.

**ULOMA.**  The same day that was the remembrance of Udo's father's, tragic death; that very day changed the fate and lives of our children for the better. From that day onwards, they realized the love that was present in their hearts for each other; they made it known to us that they want to get married, so they can be each other's **ride or die** till eternity. The best part is their 7years marriage have been blessed with three healthy boys, our grandchildren, who shares an age difference of two years each; Udoka, Udogadi and Gozie. My dear Etemma, what more can we wish for? This truly showed us that a **mother's heart and strength**, goes a long way in her child's future; try not to settle for what you feel isn't right with your child, because when you possess the will for a change, then you'll surely find a way to bring about the change, you seek.

(Uloma and Etemma, both embraced each other, so passionately like it's the last time; they truly saw reasons to be proud of each other, after achieving their desired purpose, of helping their children regain their rightful sexuality).


## ACT 10, SCENE TWENTY-SIX


**NNAMDI.**  Oh my, who am I seeing? My friend Udo; is now a full-grown man. I've truly missed you each day for the past 7years, since you were banished.

**UDO.**  If there's something I never thought I was going to see, it's definitely seeing you grow beards, Nnamdi.

**NNAMDI.**  Ha! Ha!! Ha!!! I see the sarcasm, Udo; who would have thought you'll become muscular with time?

**UDO.**  Laughing out loud! You got me there, Nnamdi.

**NNAMDI.**  But tell me, Udo; who is this beautiful lady and three big babies with you?

**UDO.**  There you got it wrong, Nnamdi; you mean my gorgeous wife and my strong sons, who are going to take after the found strength and bravery of their father.

**NNAMDI.**  I never thought I'll ever hear you say this! Udo, so you've deceived me all these years? I even stopped visiting you at a point, because I got scared you would end up raping me; seeing your lust for men back then.

**UDO.**   I'm glad you said back then, Nnamdi; if I've known that I'll be so moved by what's between a woman's legs, then I wouldn't have wasted my time admiring everything in a man, I also possess.

**NNAMDI.**   Udo, I'm so happy to hear you boldly say this, back then, when I chased after women, you were like; what's so special that attracts you to women? I guess now I don't have to tell you, for you've experienced and testified to it, yourself.

**UDO.**   Ha! Ha!! Ha!!! I just can't stop laughing, Nnamdi; by the way, hope you've settled down now? Because the way you chased after the young girls in this village; it was as if you weren't going to spare any for the young men, like myself, to add to our body count.

**NNAMDI.**   I see you know me well, my friend; I finally found love, in the midst of my lustfulness. I'm married to a woman from this village and we're blessed with two beautiful daughters; my first daughter is more or less, your eldest son's age.

**UDO.**   That's so good to hear, Nnamdi; as a man, it's important you finally settle down, after you might have played around, and it's also important that you behave more responsibly in your marriage. Well, I hope to come see you some other time; now, I'm on my way to the palace, to answer the Igwe's call.

**NNAMDI.**   Udo, just imagine how that skipped my mind; I forgot to ask you how come you are allowed back in the village, after being banished.

**UDO:**  Yes my friend, I came because the Igwe summoned me; that's why, we both crossed path on my way to the palace.

**NNAMDI:**  Go on Udo, and I hope the Igwe's call is a good one.

**Ala Umu Obodo Palace**

**PALACE GUARD:**  Igwe, the guest you're expecting has arrived; but it seems, he didn't come alone.

**IGWE:**  I made it clear to you to invite only, Udo; so how come, he came with his mother?

**PALACE GUARD:**  Igwe, I sent the message like you asked; with a clear tone, that Udo should visit the palace once again. My apologies, Igwe, I clearly didn't hear well, to invite him alone; but now I recall, I don't think he came with his mother, but a younger woman and children.

**IGWE:**  Are you trying to tell me; Udo is now married?

**PALACE GUARD:**  Though, it is a mere assumption, till we hear from the horse's mouth; my honest opinion is he's now a married man, your majesty.

**IGWE:**  Who could have thought Udo knows how to use his manhood after all? This sure amuses me, but do show him in; I have a lot to discuss with him.

(Udo followed the palace guard inside the palace, and he was received by the Igwe; to find out in person, the reason, he was summoned)

**UDO:**  Igwe, this commoner has come into your palace, as per your request to see this commoner.

**IGWE:**  Welcome back, Udo; raise your head and look at me eyeball to eyeball.

**UDO:**  As you wish, your majesty; my prin….

**IGWE:**  Why are you so startled, Udo; you don't recognize me anymore?

**UDO:**  My prince, but you went on exile with the Igwe at that time, who's also your father; how is this now possible?

**IGWE:**  You're right, Udo; the same day the royal family went on exile, was the same day, you and your mom were banished from this village.

**UDO:**  That's true, my prince; but, how is it you're back at the palace?

**IGWE:**  First of all, Udo, I'm now the Igwe of this village, as it should be; the sad part is my father passed away, just 3 years after facing exile. After going on exile due to the immature and forbidden act of mine; we all found it so hard to cope in where we found refuge. My father after dethroning himself fell into a state of severe depression. He found it so difficult to cope, each day felt like a massive torture, for he felt like he has failed his progenitors; he even felt worse, when he recalled the affliction, he unintentionally caused the people, during his reign as the king. It was indeed a turbulent time for our royal family; in this difficult period, came a reason to hold smile dearly, once again. I never knew I've gotten a maid pregnant, from my womanizing days; she gave birth to my son, who is now my heir apparent. On the 4<sup>th</sup> year of our exile, barely a year after the king couldn't carry on, but sadly gave up the ghost due to a heart attack; the Ezemmuo visited us in our place of refuge. He came as always; the mouthpiece and messenger of the gods, to deliver a message to me in person. The message was, "For the royal family to return, so I can reclaim the throne, for it's my birthright". The Ezemmuo clearly told me, I have to return; the successors of my father, all passed away just a year into their reign, so mysteriously. It's a clear sign that the throne only recognizes my lineage; the throne doesn't recognize a different clan as its head, even Ezemmuo concurred. The Ezemmuo went on to say that the child, the maid delivered for me, was destined to prove to the people of this village, that irrespective of my forbidden act; my status as a man remains unchanged as well as my sexual potency.

**UDO.**   What a true story, your majesty; but how did you come to know of your son?

**IGWE.**   Udo my man, the ways of the gods are truly not the ways of mankind; Ezemmuo saw the revelation, since he's the eyes of the gods. That was how, I came to know of it; Ezemmuo even brought my 4year old son at that time, who is now a 7-year-old prince. Together with his mother, who I owe my restoration to, if not for her meritorious deeds of nurturing my child for the long overdue time, even though, I never planned to get her pregnant, and despite my unfair treatment towards her, after I felt I've used her. She's a blessing and that's why I made her my lovely wife, and the Lolo (Queen) of my reign; I now value her in high esteem, and regard her as priceless in my life. Because, I can now show my face to my late father and our ancestors, that despite the shame I brought to the royal lineage, I still regained, "What is rightfully ours".

**UDO:**  Igwe, huge congratulations from myself and my family; you indeed restored what is rightfully yours and your ancestry's. Also Igwe, pardon my contemptuous tongue; but I dare to say that the prince and my eldest son are age mates.

**IGWE:**  Thank you for the sincere congratulations. And about the age mates stuff; it's even more flattering to hear. However; I called you here for two main reasons. First off, I want to apologize to you for the forbidden plot, I got you involved in; It might be considered unthinkable for a king to apologize to a commoner, even when he has done wrong, but not this king. Will you forgive me, Udo?

**UDO:**  Your majesty, I am nothing but your slave, you owe me no apology at all, but only your command, am I expected to follow. For me, a thing of the past, remains a thing for the past, and shouldn't be brought to the present, or future; for it has taught the lesson that it was supposed to teach. Igwe, we've learnt from the forbidden plot, and it is evidently an experience, that should never be revisited.

**IGWE:**  Udo, you haven't just regained your manliness, but you also regained the wisdom that completes you as a man; for you reason and make wise use of your words.

**UDO:**  It is an honor of this commoner, to be complimented by you, Igwe.

**IGWE.**  My second and final reason for inviting you over is because, **"You and your mother's banishment have been uplifted"**, and therefore stands no more. I can imagine you're wondering; how this is also possible?

**UDO.**  You took the words out of my mouth, your majesty; please bring me out of my robe of suspense.

**IGWE.**  You can bank on it, Udo; I had a private discussion with Ezemmuo, couple of years ago, after my coronation as the Igwe; where I asked if it's possible for you to also return to this village, putting an indefinite end to your banishment? Ezemmuo made it clear that you portrayed yourself as a **bad seed**, which endangers the roots of the plantation, and as such it has to be cut off; to prevent a bad harvest of the season. What he meant by that is, though I am not homosexual, you on the other hand showed signs that would make a witness of your behaviors, describe you as homosexual; which is a good enough reason to take you away from the people of this land, before it constitutes a forbidden plot all over the village that will have a disastrous end for the entire village. And the only way Udo can return; is when he has a family of his own as a man, he is. To be honest, I kept tails on you for the past couple of years, but I was still unable to locate your hideout; till, I visited the neighboring village last week to watch the final Mgba (wrestling) of two aggressors, whom people brag to be the two best fighters in the neighboring villages and beyond. I was so shocked to see

that you were not just one of the two best fighters, but you even cemented your legacy by coming out victorious; you are now the best fighter in the villages and beyond. I found out your location, all thanks to your popularity. Congratulations! Moving on, Udo, I need not ask at this point, for it's obvious that this is your wife and children that accompanied you over here; am I right after all?

**UDO:**  Yes Igwe, you speak nothing but the truth and I'm honored by your congratulatory gesture, for it means a lot to me; I'm also proud to say I'm no girly anymore. I started wrestling since I recovered my manliness; I became ambitious, because all the weaknesses I possessed over the years, turned into strength, which I wished to show to the people and also prove to them that, I've moved from the weakest boy I've been known to be, and, I wanted to become the strongest man that will make his fellow men tremble, and admire them no more. I accomplished this feat, like I intended; by defeating every challenger from all the neighboring villages, to be crowned, **"The strongest man alive"**. I'm also a changed family man. My life changed completely for the best, seven (7) years ago; the same date with the tragic passing of my late father, although, many years before. That same night of the same day, seven years ago; was when I made love to a woman, who is now my wife, for the very first time in my life. The most magical thing about this is my wife was also sexually active only to her gender; we both felt the greatest touch on the same day, after our first love making, which remains **unforgettable.** Our first child was also born that year, when my wife became pregnant after our several sexual escapades from that day onwards; our first son is 7years old, second is 5years old, and the third is 3 and counting. The best part, Igwe; is I have no plans of slowing down, for I'm now sexually active and I will keep on, *"knacking"*, till I add the title of, "Father of all Nations", to my achieved status.

**IGWE.** That's hilarious! In my lifetime; I never thought, I'll ever hear you utter
this statement. Who knows; I could even give my daughter's hand in
marriage to one of your sons, as soon as the expectant Queen puts to bed.
Our second child is kicking in the stomach of my Lolo; my instinct tells me
it's a female child, and my instinct is never wrong.

**UDO.** The Igwe is so kind to hold this commoner in high esteem; my family and
I, are honored and forever grateful, your majesty.

**GOLLIBE.** Do accept our condolences for the demise of your father, the
former Igwe, since sadly we weren't present, when he kicked the
bucket, four years ago; like I heard you say.

**IGWE.** Hearing how angelic you sound; I see that my friend, Udo, chose the
right woman to spend the rest of his life with. I and my mother and sisters
haven't found it easy to cope without his presence, but however no one can
alter fate; that's why we simply have to move on, no matter how big of a
loss, one might face. Come on in, Udo; I'll like you to say a word or two to
the elders, and members of my cabinet.

**UDO.** Please lead the way, your majesty, for we shall follow.


(Udo, ran into his mom's uncle in the palace, who pleaded to have an audience
with him, and he assented)

**DEDE.** Udo, can I have a word with you?

**UDO.** Of course, Nna anyi; you're still a father to my mother and grandfather to
me, and also a great-grandfather to my children.

**DEDE.**  Udo, you mean you now have children of your own?

**UDO.**  Yes, Nna anyi; I can proudly say this Udo in your presence is a full grown family man, and not the girly Udo, you once knew.

**DEDE.**  Are you for real, my child?

**UDO.**  I've never lied to your frightening face before, so I won't start now, Nna anyi.

**DEDE.**  Udo, I've haven't been myself since the day, you and your mother were banished; I felt so guilty that I'd even wished for my death, but it wasn't forthcoming. Udo, please, will you forgive me for wanting to have you killed back then?

**UDO.**  To err is human, to forgive is divine; at the end of the day, one has to let go and not hold grudges, which could end up eating your peace for life. I forgive you for nothing, Nna anyi; for I've never had anything in mind against you.

**DEDE.**  Change is indeed constant; who would have thought you'll grow and mature into a Wiseman, judging from the cowardly acts, you exhibited in your teenage and youthful days?

**UDO.**  It is what it is, Nna anyi. No man can be denied redemption, as long as he sees the wrong; he wants to change to his right. I'm that man; all I want to do now, is show the people that despite, "Who I was seen as, I can still become who I was made to be".

**DEDE.**  You speak no ordinary words, but spit out a life-changing vision, that
mankind needs to hear and digest; I never thought I'll say this, but I'm so
proud of the man, you've become, Udo.

**UDO.**  If there's something I wish to hear so dearly from you, Nna anyi; that's
your words of praise, upon me. I am now honored and more fulfilled to
hear you speak in a way, that shows you accept me as descendant of your
lineage; my maternal ancestors must have accepted me as well, with pride.

**DEDE.**  Udo, may the gods of our land bless your family; your wife and children
have my blessings also.

**UDO.**  Nna anyi, regardless of how proud a man might have become, it is also
important that he knows when to, **"Show gratitude"**; thank you, Nna anyi.
Let's go in and join Igwe, because it is wrong and unacceptable to keep
a king waiting.

(Udo went in to join the king and the elders, who were present in the palace;
unknowing to him, there was an unexpected chaos)

**IGWE.**  Udo, we have a scene outside; which I don't know how to deal with.

**UDO.**  Please speak to me, your majesty; for this servant holds your worries, as
his as well.

**IGWE.**  It seems, words got out and the people found out in an unplanned way;
that you've returned to this village, and now, there's ruckus out there.

**UDO:**  Igwe, give me your royal command, to go out there and speak to the people; if after that, I'm still not accepted in this village, then I shall take my family and leave at once, and we'll never turn back nor come back again.

**IGWE:**  Though, I fear they might not want to hear you out, Udo; I give you my royal command to make peace with the people, so you and your family can come back, like you never left. For, **"There's no place like home"**.


## ACT 10, SCENE TWENTY-SEVEN


**UDO:**  Ndewo Ndi Obodo Anyi (it is a way of greeting the people of the village). Aha m bu, Udo (it means; my name is Udo, in the lingo used), enwerem ihe m nwere ikwu, biko gee m nti (it means; I have something to say and please listen to me, in the lingo used). (The reaction Udo got from the people was indeed scary, because they acted so furiously to see him back in the village, because of the forbidden plot, he was involved in). (However, Udo neither showed fear nor signs of holding back his words). I stand before the people of this village, ready to be stoned to death, as long as my voice is heard. I'm not going to show signs of giving up on this speech that I know have my fate on the line; if I can ever be allowed back into this village with my family members, or face banishment forever. I brought my family here today, because I came prepared to prove my potency as a man, no matter what it takes; if y'all doubt my sexual activeness as a man, trust me, I'll make love to my wife in your presence, but not any other woman. If there is something I've come to realize in life; it is the fact that any action we carryout, is either an experience which is going to teach others, or a lesson, we learn ourselves. Trust me when I say, I won't mind repeating the forbidden plot, I was involved in, as long as I'm certain that it will help the future generations avoid repeating such forbidden act, which cost me so dearly; for I lost the right to live among the people, and the right to call the home of my forefathers, my own home. It is easy for people to judge you when you've done something wrong, just because they aren't the ones on

the

receiving end. How hypocritical! It's easy for everyone to march to the palace with hope that they make it clear, that their delight is in my own death, or my rights to live in my place of birth and hometown, permanently. How unfair! It is easy to wish for the downfall of your brother or sister, all because you saw their flaws, forgetting, that most of you commit atrocious crimes, which you hide from the eyes of everyone; but you forget to realize that the gods sees everything we all do, including who has the pure or evil heart. How common of mankind! Most of you weep so bitterly when you experience the demise of a loved one, but yet, you see reasons to celebrate after witnessing others lose their own loved ones due to your wicked plot; and then you're quick to tell people that are willing to help others mourn, that they should allow anyone affected, bury their dead, meanwhile, you needed people's support during your own time of mourning. How normal of people! I don't have an issue with anyone that insists that I don't deserve a second chance; but you must say before everyone, if you've lived a perfect life, without you making mistakes or actions that warrant punishment. Please step forward; if truly you're

exempted of mistakes, and you're indeed a perfect human being. Funny, no one is coming out right? It's easy to leave your own home and come to the palace, just to chant, "Udo must die"! It's also easy to say, "Udo is a forbidden child"! Meanwhile, you feel you aren't the victim, and as such, "The actual victim deserves no second chance"; because you are now the creator and chief judge of mankind, right? It's high time, people realizes that
irrespective of the position or status, you've achieved in life; you still remain
a creature, like everyone you feel is beneath you, including animals. As far as I'm concerned, I'm in support of the fact that everyone deserves a second chance, regardless of the forbidden plot, they might have been involved in; if a person commits the same crime, after being granted a second chance, then that shows, they aren't ready to seek change, for they see nothing wrong in what they've actually done, or the misery they caused. And trust me, when I say, if such person that sees no wrong in his or her actions, faces
punishment; then the people or prosecutor will feel less guilty, because the offender posed as a threat to the community. Just imagine, how it felt for me
to be banished, knowing full well, that I was so weak to challenge my own genes, which at that time; found sexual desires only in my fellow man. I tried personally to fight and overcome the desires, but they kept coming way stronger on me; if it's not for the bravery and fearless hearts of my mother and my wife's mother, I don't think I'll be a saved and changed man, that I am now. Please forgive me my people; I was a victim that was

described as **the bad seed**, because I posed as a threat to the root of the plantation, which is the people and this village in general; due to the abnormal behaviors, I portrayed. Forgive me my people; for the hidden tears, my mother cries out every midnight since we were banished, still haunts me every day of my existence. Please forgive me, my people; because I've done nothing but make excuses, every time my sons asked me, "Is this place we stay, our village"? The place happens to be the village of my wife, and their maternal home, but in actual fact, it isn't their village; because their village is supposed to be their father's hometown. And lastly, please forgive me, my people; because if you don't, I will never be able to find rest or peace in my grave, no matter how decorated and luxurious, it might

look,

when I finally join my ancestors. For I know I'll be faced with the wrath of my ancestors as my punishment, for bringing shame to our long lasting lineage. At the end, I still accept the fact that I remain the **protagonist** of this, **"FORBIDDEN PLOT"**.


DO YOU THINK, UDO, DESERVES TO BE FORGIVEN BY HIS PEOPLE, AND SO, HE AND HIS FAMILY SHOULD BE GRANTED A SECOND CHANCE AND ACCEPTED BACK IN THE VILLAGE?


THE END.